FINDING LOVE

RACHEL HANNA

*A*ddison sat on the bed in her old room and remembered her younger years. Her walls were still painted a pale shade of pink, and her cheer-leading trophies still adorned the shelves on the walls next to the closet.

She wasn't quite the baby of the Parker family, but her brothers all watched over her as if she was. She felt bad for snapping at Jackson recently, but she was mentally and physically tired these days. And her brother could take it. He always took the brunt of her mood swings, being that he was like a father figure to her anyway.

Addison had only been four years old when she lost her father, so she had never really known the love of a Dad. Since her mother never remarried, she didn't have that fatherly bond with anyone except Jackson. He had headed up their family in such a responsible way, and she was sure their father was proud of him. It occurred to her that she'd never told her brother that, and he would most certainly appreciate it. Just another thing on her "to-do" list.

She wasn't used to feeling afraid. Even as a child, she was surrounded by her four brothers anytime she needed something. A close knit family, the Parkers survived the death of their father and continued to thrive despite every obstacle thrown their way.

She had watched her mother, Adele, overcome the loss of her husband, raise five children and build a business that had become a cornerstone in January Cove. The coastal Georgia town was her home, and she loved being back, although she had run out into the big world of interior design as soon as she was old enough.

Addison was the wild child of the family. Always had been. She was what most people would call a "free spirit", and she craved a big life outside of the small town of January Cove. She wanted to be known for something, and she longed to use the creativity she had brimming from every pore of her being.

She was forever embarrassing her mother with her childhood antics such as toilet papering the principal's house in high school, organizing a student sit-in to oppose the new dress code rules and even writing letters to the editor of the local newspaper with her views on just about every political decision in their town. Addison wanted her voice to be heard, and her ideas to be known. She had big dreams and an even bigger plan for her life.

As soon as she was old enough, she went to school to be an interior designer and headed off to Atlanta to make it big. Her mother was her role model, and she wanted to succeed just like her. But her plans were derailed.

At first, things went well. She became known for her superior sense of style as she decorated houses all over the Atlanta area. One of her living room designs was even featured in the local newspaper in the lifestyle section. She'd sent a copy of the spread to her mother who bragged about her all over January Cove for days.

When she met Jim, she'd been in Atlanta for about eighteen months. A client introduced her to him at a charity fundraiser, and she was taken with him from the start. He was an up and coming attorney who had just moved to Atlanta from New York. He was nothing like the guys she'd dated in the past, especially given the fact that he had a thick Northern accent and she was the epitome of a Southern belle. Well, a quirky Southern belle. She liked to think of herself as Scarlett O'Hara but without the hoop skirt.

They'd fallen in love hard and fast. Within six months, she found herself walking down the aisle at a small chapel on the outskirts of the north Georgia mountains. Her family didn't make the wedding as Jim really wanted it to be a small affair with just the two of them, a minister and their witnesses. It wasn't what she'd dreamed of as a little girl, but she had convinced herself that the wedding wasn't important. The marriage was her focus, and she wanted it to be perfect.

So, she went to work making herself into the perfect wife. They bought a house in an upscale neighborhood and started getting involved in the Atlanta lifestyle. They belonged to all the most prestigious clubs, and Addison found herself getting further removed from interior design while Jim's name was known all over town for his lethal skills as an attorney.

Whenever she spoke to her mother or one of her brothers, she pretended all was well. As far as they were concerned, she and her husband were jet setters, flying all over the world enjoying the finest of accommodations. In reality, she spent a lot of her time alone, cleaning their large empty house and waiting for her husband to come home. She was too proud and too embarrassed to tell her family about her loneliness, not because they would say, "I told you so", but because they would worry. And she never wanted to worry the people she loved most.

Jim worked all the time, and he often traveled alone and stayed late at the office. She tried to be understanding because he was building a business after all, but it was hard. Trying to create the perfect marriage alone was impossible, and talking to a man who debated others for a living was far too tiring for Addison.

What bothered her most of all was how different she was becoming. Her personality was squashed, and her dreams seemed lost in the wind. Everything she had dreamed of - and the reason she left January Cove - was gone. She was stuck in a lonely marriage with a man who seemed incapable of loving her the way she needed to be loved. She was occasional arm candy at fundraisers and company dinners, but she was otherwise a single woman in a large house.

She wasn't as close to her family anymore either, and that broke her heart. Looking back, she couldn't figure out where she had gone so wrong to completely screw up her life so badly. Her family was her rock, and they had been through so much. Coming home to January Cove had not only been about trying to figure out what to do about her situation, but also to reconnect with her brothers and mother. She hoped she could repair what had been lost over the last few years.

The ocean offered her a sense of calm that couldn't be matched by anything else. All the yoga and meditation in the world - something she did in Atlanta - would never equal the sound of the waves crashing into the shore over and over.

Talking to her family about what had happened to her was going to be difficult, and she needed some down time to get her mind clear. She was tired lately, so waking up at six in the morning was challenging but necessary. As she slipped out the front door, the sun was just pecking over the dunes across the street from the Parker home.

Her long, flowing dress blew in the ocean breeze as she walked down to her favorite spot. She had wonderful memories of playing volleyball with her brothers and building sandcastles with Aaron when they were younger.

She slid down onto the sand and pulled her knees up. Wiggling her toes in the sand felt like heaven, even as the cooler temperatures whipped into her face. The smell of the salty sea air was a welcome departure from the smoggy conditions she was used to in recent years. There were no car horns honking, just the sound of sea gulls and waves lapping the beach.

While she loved big city life at first, she would never admit to her family that she missed home. She loved her career, but she loved January Cove more. Still, coming back would have seemed like failure to her, even though she was one hundred percent sure her family would have welcomed her with open arms. That's just who they were. They were her rock, and for some reason she'd avoided their support in recent years.

Maybe it was her pride. Her mother had always said she was just like her father, although she didn't remember him really. She was only four when he died, so her recollections were muddled at best. She had often tried to dig deep within her soul to draw out any little memories of her father. Maybe the sound of his laughter or the smell of his cologne. But she never could remember anything. All she had to go on were old photographs her mother had shown her from time to time.

Addison always dreaded Father's Day when she was in school. She was supposed to be "Daddy's girl". As the only daughter in their group of five kids, it had been her right and privilege to be "Daddy's girl", but that had been taken from her at such a young age. Even now, there was a pain in her heart where her father should have been, and she wondered how that factored in to her choice of Jim as her husband.

From all she'd been told, Jim was nothing like her father. Her Dad had been kind and caring and attentive to her mother and siblings. Jim had turned out to be none of those things. But maybe she had been looking for a strong male figure in her life? She didn't know, and she had spent so much time lamenting her choice in husbands that her head hurt.

A lone sea gull flew overhead as the sun continued to make its ascent over the horizon. She stared up at it, but caught a person's face instead.

"Jackson!" she said, holding a hand to her chest as she tried to calm her pounding heart. "Good Lord! You scared me to death!" She was half angry and half relieved that she wasn't alone - and that he wasn't an axe murderer.

"Sorry, sis," he said laughing as she reached out and slapped his leg.

"What are you doing here?" Jackson eased down beside her.

"Well, I come down here every morning. This is where I do my yoga and tai chi."

Addison stared at him for a moment before he broke into laughter again. Jackson's jokes left a lot to be desired, especially so early in the morning.

"Seriously, were you following me?"

"Oh, get over yourself. I do come down here every morning because this is where I have my coffee," he said holding up a thermal mug. "You know I've always been an early riser. But you... um, no. You've never been an early riser, so what gives?"

"Things change, Jackson. People change." As soon as

she said it, she regretted it. After all, Jackson had practically raised her, and he knew her better than she knew herself.

He studied her carefully for a moment. "I suppose that's true. I mean, look at me."

"What are you talking about?"

"Well, just a few weeks ago, I was sitting behind a desk, piled high with papers, focused on work. Now, I'm in love with a wonderful woman and living most of the time in January Cove. Things can sure change rapidly…"

"I'm so happy for you, Jackson. Really, I am. No one deserves happiness more than you do, big brother," she said, chucking her shoulder against his. She really believed what she'd said. Jackson had been the strong rock that she'd needed throughout her growing up years. He checked out boyfriends, set bullies straight and even took her to father/daughter dances at school.

"You deserve to be happy too, Addy," he said, calling her by her shortened nickname.

"What makes you think I'm not happy now?"

"Because I know you, and I've played poker with you. And you have a terrible poker face." She laughed and pinched his leg causing him to jump and wince.

"Jackson, I just need some time…"

"Time to do what? Look, Addy, whatever this thing is, it isn't going to get better by you keeping it bottled up. You look like hell."

"Thanks a lot!"

"Well, it's true. You know I've always been honest with you, and you don't look like yourself. You look tired. Actually, you look exhausted. It's worrying me, and I know it's worrying Mom. Let us help you."

She looked at him for a moment and took a deep breath before putting her forehead on her knees. Being vulnerable was never her strong suit. She preferred to keep a smile on her face at all times. "Smile. It makes people wonder what you're up to" was her motto.

Jackson sat there quietly, and Addison knew it was because he was sure she was about to break.

"Okay, I'll tell you... all of you... but I want to do it as a family. I don't want to have to repeat myself over and over. Can you get everyone together?"

"How about lunch?"

"Sounds like a plan. Now, do you mind giving me a little time? You know, to gather my thoughts?"

Jackson nodded, stood and kissed her on the top of her head before he quietly walked away. A single tear fell down Addison's cheek as she felt the love of her older brother and simultaneously felt the weight of shame she was about to place on her beloved family.

CHAPTER 2

The smell of Christmas was already in the air in the Parker household. With a fresh Christmas tree sitting undecorated in the front hall, Addison flashed back in her mind to the many Christmases that she and her brothers would drag decorations down from the attic to make the house look like a Norman Rockwell painting.

Her mother had always made everything seem perfect, although as an adult Addison now realized that her mother had probably been lonely herself. She never dated around the kids, and she poured her whole soul into her children and her work. She made holidays fun and memorable as all of her kids grew up and found lives of their own. She had been like a lighthouse out in the ocean, steering her children to good lives and happiness, while she remained stuck in the same place year after year. It made Addison a little sad to think about.

The last few years in Addison's large home had

made Christmas feel hollow. With a plastic tree - Jim was allergic to the real thing - and expensive decorations, Christmas had never felt the same. There was no depth of love in her house. No kids. No pets. Often no husband. But here, love oozed from the walls, it seemed.

Hosting Christmas parties for clients and other attorneys had been tedious at best. Making sure she had the right crystal glasses and the most expensive wines available. Using her best fake smile, she wined and dined everyone from congressmen to law partners all in an effort to make her husband look good.

As she walked into the family room, everyone was already gathered waiting for her. Laughter stopped as she entered the room, and an abnormal hush fell over everyone. It was all so serious, and she hated serious moments. She had accidentally laughed at her great aunt Gertrude's funeral when she was sixteen simply because serious stuff made her nervous, and she laughed when she was nervous. This time, she had no desire to laugh and was holding back tears already.

"Hi, sweetie," Adele said walking to her daughter and pushing a strand of her hair behind her ear. "Everyone is here. Jackson said..."

"Yes, I wanted to talk to all of you," Addison was happy to see that it was just her mother and her brothers. No fiancees, no girlfriends, no one to possibly judge her.

"It's okay, sis. We're here for you, whatever it is..." Aaron said. The youngest of their brood, Aaron had been her close companion when they were kids. They were only two years apart in age, and she loved playing with him when they were growing up. He was outdoorsy, and her love of adventure matched his personality very well.

Addison slid slowly into an overstuffed arm chair in the corner and took a deep breath before meeting her mother's eyes. Adele sat down next to Brad on the sofa, and Jackson slipped his arm around her from the other side.

"Okay…" Addison started. "I've called you all here because I need to explain some things. I'm sure it's obvious to all of you that something has been up with me for a few weeks now."

"Yes, honey. We've all been worried about you," Adele said nodding her head.

"I know, Mom, and I'm sorry. I just had to work some things out in my own time."

"We understand, Addy. Just tell us…" Kyle said, obviously growing impatient in his concern for his sister.

"Last year, Jim had an affair," she blurted out a little more quickly than she would have liked.

"That son of a…" Jackson said through gritted teeth.

"Jackson!" Adele chided. "Language."

"Sorry, Mom," he said rubbing his hand hard against his mouth in an effort to stifle some other choice words.

"It was with his assistant. Tiffani with an 'i,'" Addison said rolling her eyes. "Hot young blonde, just out of college."

"Dear God," Kyle muttered under his breath as he

got up to join Jackson in pacing the room like two caged tigers.

"Anyway, I found out when he left his secondary cell phone out by accident."

"Secondary cell phone?" Adele said.

"Yes. He was very good at covering his tracks for the most part. Tiffani would travel with him, unbeknownst to me, of course."

"I thought you were traveling with him?" Adele said.

"Most of the time, I was home alone. I just told you that I was traveling because, well, I was ashamed at the state of our marriage. I wanted so badly to make it work, so I did my best to make it look perfect."

"Oh, sweetie, you could have come to any of us…"

"I know, Mom. This wasn't about any of you. It was about my own foolish pride, I suppose."

"So you left him last year?" Brad asked.

"No. I confronted him, and we went to marriage counseling. But he would stand me up at our counseling appointments, and the affair probably continued. I don't really know. Eventually, Tiffani moved on to another attorney in the office and Jim came crawling back to me. That lasted all of two months before he started leaving me home alone again. I realized nothing was going to change, so I moved out last summer."

"Last summer? Where have you been living?" Jackson asked.

"I got a small apartment and started divorce proceedings which isn't the easiest thing when your soon to be ex husband is an attorney. It became really clear that I was going to get the shaft. My interior design business has been floundering since we married, and he was smearing my name all over town. I couldn't get work… so…"

"So?" Adele said, now sitting on the edge of her seat.

"I started bartending."

"Bartending? Oh my word!" Adele covered her mouth as if Addison had just admitted to prostitution.

"Mom…" Jackson said shaking his head.

"I'm sorry, honey. I just wasn't expecting that…"

"It's okay, Mom. I know it's not a line of work you'd be proud of. Not for me anyway. And it's not what I want to do either."

"I still don't get why you didn't just come home, sis?" Kyle said.

"Because there's more to the story. You see, I met someone while I was tending bar. Seemed like a nice guy. He was a home builder, owned his own company, treated me great. We went on a few dates and I just wanted someone who wanted me…" Tears started to fall from her eyes. "Jim never really wanted me. He just needed arm candy for social functions, but he was never my friend."

"And this man was your friend?" Aaron asked.

"I thought so, but my mindset at the time wasn't good. I was strapped for money, exhausted from work and Jim was raking me over the coals in our divorce. I just fell into the arms of the first nice guy I met, and that was Eric."

"So where is this Eric?" Jackson demanded to know, his arms crossed against his broad chest.

"I don't know. I haven't seen him in weeks."

"I don't get why you're telling us this, sweetie..."

"I'm pregnant, Mom. I'm carrying Eric's baby and he wants no part of it." Addison sobbed into her hands as Jackson immediately knelt at her side. Adele held her hand over her mouth again, and Brad pulled her in close to him for support. No one wanted her to have another mini stroke.

"It's going to be okay, Addy. We're here for you," Jackson soothed.

"No! Don't you understand? I have no job, no career, no home really. Yet I have a baby on the way. I'm four months along, and Jim has taken everything we built together. I have nothing to offer a baby, but here I am in this situation. I'm caught. And now I'm going to bring shame to my whole family!"

"No, honey, we would never be ashamed of you," Adele said as she stood and knelt in front of her daughter. "This isn't the 1950s, Addison Rose. Women have babies without being married all the time. You're a strong woman, and you're going to be a strong mother. We will help you."

Addison looked into her mother's tear stained eyes and knew she was speaking from her heart. "But this isn't what you wanted for me, Mom. And I know that."

"Truthfully, no. But not because I'm ashamed. It's because I want the easiest roads for all of my children, and this isn't going to be an easy road. But we will walk it together, Addison. You're not alone."

All of the brothers surrounded their only sister and pulled her into a big family hug. Never had she felt more love. Never had she felt more ashamed of herself.

"Okay, enough with the crying," Adele said as she stood up and wiped her eyes. "We have a house to decorate!"

"But, Mom, what about…" Addison said, pointing down to her ever enlarging belly. It seemed bigger now that everyone knew, although it was still barely noticeable. Thank goodness it was winter and big sweater weather.

"Sweetie, we'll deal with that in time. For now, we must decorate for a Parker family Christmas. And we must make you an appointment with Dr. Sylvan. You will get the best in prenatal care. This is my first grand baby, after all!" She smiled widely, and it made Addison feel a little better.

Addison was always amazed at her mother's ability not to wallow in bad news. It was a skill she had honed since losing the love of her life. She supposed it was a skill she too would need to learn as being a single mother wasn't going to be easy.

Adele would often say things like "Don't wallow, sweetie. It makes your face ugly." Addison almost laughed thinking about it. The epitome of Southern grace, Adele Parker had not let anything life threw at her get her down. She had always picked herself up and carried on with it.

"Well, then I guess we'd better start decorating," Addison said as she wiped her eyes. Jackson threw his arm around her as they walked into the foyer.

"You know, sis, if this is a boy, I really like the name Jack." He smiled at her as she cast him a knowing glance.

"I was thinking I liked the name Aaron better," she said playfully.

"Yes!" Aaron yelled from behind.

For the first time in weeks, Addison felt at home. At peace. Like things might be okay. So she allowed herself to decorate the house for Christmas without thinking too hard about what was coming next. Like her Southern belle idol, Scarlett O'Hara, she would think about that another day.

~

THERE SEEMED to be hundreds of white dresses in the shop, and they were all starting to look alike to Addison. She had promised her sister-in-law to be, Jenna, that she would help her pick out the perfect gown for her spring wedding to Kyle. But right now she was wishing that she'd stayed home because these brides were crazy.

It was the annual bridal gown "Christmas Crazy" sale at the Bridal Warehouse just outside of January Cove. Hundreds of women descended on the large warehouse one day per year to get "sales even Santa himself couldn't get". The advertising surrounding the event made Addison laugh, but Jenna was totally serious. She had a certain gown she wanted, and no one would get in her way.

"Okay, when they open the door, I'll go left and you go right," Jenna had instructed as they stood in line just before 8 AM. "The dress is white..."

17

"I would assume so," Addison said, laughing and rolling her eyes. Jenna was not amused.

"Do you hate me?" Jenna said, poking her lip out in mock offense.

"Of course not. You're like a true sister to me, Jenna. We've known each other a long time. But this is a side of you I haven't seen before. Crazy Bride Commando," Addison said giggling. "You're kind of scary. I'll have to pray for my brother."

Addison had been raised around Jenna since she and Kyle were high school sweethearts. Although they took a long detour in their relationship, Addison was thrilled when Kyle reconnected with the love of his life. And now he was helping raise Jenna's little girl, and they were so happy.

"Sorry, Addy. I'm just so excited to marry your brother. It's been a long road, you know that."

"You guys are so in love," Addison said. "I'm a little jealous of that."

Jenna put her hands on Addison's shoulders and smiled. "You're going to get through this, Addy. You are a strong woman, just like your momma. And you will find happiness. Somewhere out there is a man who is meant just for you, and he will raise your child with you just like Kyle is doing for me. You have to believe that."

"I want to, but right now I can't focus on a man. I have to figure out what to do about this," she said pointing down at her ever growing midsection. "I was ready for kids, but not alone. I don't know how I'll ever do this."

"You'd be surprised at the things you can do when you have to," Jenna said. "You're the spunkiest, funniest gal I know, and this baby is going to be lucky to have you as his or her mother."

Addison smiled appreciatively, but inside she knew that she was keeping another secret that would likely destroy how her family thought of her yet again.

~

"I swear, there is no place on earth that has better cheese fries than Zach's," Addison said as she shoveled more of the delectable fries into her mouth. Eating for two was turning out to be a lot of fun in her mind.

"I know. And this milkshake is going to keep me from fitting into my new dress if I keep this up," Jenna said with a laugh.

The morning turned out not to be so bad after all. Jenna walked straight into the warehouse and located her dress within minutes. It was a larger size, but she would have it altered closer to the wedding.

"You're going to be such a beautiful bride, Jen," Addison said as she took a sip of her own milkshake.

"I want to take your brother's breath away. Then I will know I've done my job," she said grinning.

"Well, from what I can tell, you pretty much take his breath away everyday," Addison said. "And sometimes I want to tell ya'll to get a room!"

The women laughed, so loudly that they were afraid they'd get thrown out of Zach's. Instead, they drew the attention of Rebecca and Tessa who were walking in to eat.

"Hey, ladies!" Tessa said as they approached the table. "We didn't know ya'll would be here."

"Wedding dress shopping this morning," Jenna said.

"Well, where is it?" Rebecca asked with a large smile.

"Oh, in the car under lock and key!" Addison said, pushing out one of the extra chairs with her foot. "Have a seat."

The four Parker women - well, three of them unofficial Parker women - sat there for an hour talking and laughing. Addison felt so comfortable around all of them, even though she had only recently met two of them.

"So, Addison, have you had any morning sickness?" Rebecca finally asked, making her the first person to point out the elephant in the room. Okay, maybe that was a bad pun.

"Not a lot, actually. But I've been very tired, mentally and physically."

"That means a girl!" Jenna exclaimed, clapping her hands and giggling.

"How does that mean a girl?"

"No nausea, tired... Those were main symptoms when I was pregnant with Kaitlyn."

"Not very scientific, Jenna," Addison said rolling her eyes.

"Well, she might be on to something because I was terribly sick with Leo," Rebecca said taking a sip of her drink.

"Aren't those old wives' tales?" Addison asked with a laugh.

"Sometimes those old wives knew what they were talking about!" Jenna said giggling.

"Have you heard anything from Jim?" Jenna asked softly.

Hearing his name was like having a knife shoved into her gut. She wanted to wipe that part of her past clean, but she knew she never would. How could he have deceived her so well that she didn't know she was married to a cheater?

"No. But I don't plan to. I hear from his attorney friend, Neil. Biggest worm I've ever met," Addison said.

"When will the divorce be final?"

"Probably not for at least a few more weeks. He's fighting with everything he has no to let me have anything. I literally walked away with my clothes."

"That's crazy! He's the one who cheated!" Rebecca said a little too loudly. "Sorry," she said, looking around in embarrassment.

"I know. But for now I just need to spend time with my family and find a job so I can take care of myself. I didn't come here to sponge off my mother and brothers."

"They don't mind taking care of you for awhile, Addy. They love you," Jenna said, reaching across the table and holding Addison's hand.

"I know they don't mind, but I do. I'm a grown woman who made a stupid decision, and I need to buck up and take care of myself."

"Wow, you sound just like Adele," Tessa said with a laugh. "Must be those strong Parker female genes."

"I suppose so," Addison responded, smiling at the comparison to her beloved mother. "If I can only be half the woman she is…"

"You're going to do fine, sweetie. We're all here for you," Jenna said. "Look, I know better than anyone how hard it is to raise a child alone."

"Um, so do I…." Rebecca chimed in, raising her hand.

"Hello?" Tessa said laughing.

"Wow, I guess you all know," Addison said, suddenly realizing that her table was filled with strong women who rose up during tough circumstances.

"You know, if you're looking for a part-time job, I know where you can find one," Rebecca said.

"Really? Where?"

"At Jolt!"

"Your coffee shop?" Addison asked.

"Yep. I am exhausted, and I really need someone to take the morning shifts. I am not a morning person, and I'm so busy getting Leo off the school."

"Are you sure this isn't a charity case kind of thing?" Addison asked with a sly smile.

"No! I was honestly about to put an ad in The Cove Chronicle," Rebecca said, referring to the town's newspaper. Run by one of the oldest residents of January Cove, Clifford Applebaum, The Cove Chronicle had been around for over fifty years. Not many people read it, but Clifford wasn't about to give up to that old "electronic mumbo jumbo" - his description of the Internet.

"Well, if you're serious, I would love to work at Jolt!" Addison said, excited at her first chance at making a normal life for herself. "When should I start?"

"How about tomorrow at eight?"

Addison reached across the table to shake Rebecca's hand. "You've got yourself a deal!"

"Don't you want to know the pay?" Tessa prodded. "She might be planning to work you for three pennies an hour!"

The women all laughed, and Addison took a deep breath, ready to start a whole new future.

CHAPTER 3

"Mother, honestly I don't think we need to release doves," Kyle said, rolling his eyes up in his head as he watched his mother make the third fruitcake of the evening.

"Kyle, doves would be lovely. Think of it. You'll be married on the beach with one hundred doves released into the spring sky…"

"We see a hundred seagulls everyday! No doves!" Kyle yelled playfully as he stole a cherry from one of the bowls on the kitchen counter. Never mind that he'd considered releasing doves when he proposed to Jenna but was talked out of it by Jackson.

"And we may not marry on the beach, Adele," Jenna spoke up. "I was thinking about checking into renting the old Carver plantation."

"Really?"

"Well, I just love that old place, and the grounds are spectacular in the spring," Jenna said, grinning from ear to ear. "Plus, they have that grand ballroom in the back that old man Carver added in the fifties, remember?"

"Oh yes. That would be lovely, dear."

"We had our prom there, didn't we?" Kyle asked as he snatched another cherry, and Adele popped his hand with her spoon.

"Yes, Kyle. Jeez, I'm surprised you remember that," Jenna said rolling her eyes. "Another option is marrying on the ferry. We thought it might be fun to marry there and then have our reception out on the island."

"Maybe putting more money into the reception than the wedding would be a good idea because it's always the party you remember most anyway," Kyle said with a big grin. "And the honeymoon, of course." Jenna rolled her eyes.

"Where is Miss Kaitlyn tonight, by the way?" Adele asked, changing the subject off the honeymoon as quickly as possible.

"She's sleeping over at a friend's. It's her first slumber party," Jenna said. "My girl is growing up."

"They grow up awfully fast," Adele said with a solemn look on her face. "You'll learn that soon, Addison," she said as her daughter walked into the kitchen.

"Learn what?"

"That kids grow up so fast. Why, one moment you're holding them in your arms and the next minute they're holding their own kids." Adele sighed. "Such is the circle of life, I guess."

Addison's stomach churned. What would her family think of her when she told them her other news?

"Can I help with dinner?" Addison asked.

"No, honey, it's all ready. I was just getting a few more fruitcakes going. You know how my agents and customers love them," Adele said, and it was true. Her fruitcakes were famous in January Cove, and she loved the attention every Christmas. She put something in them that no one else did because people ate them up. Adele claimed the extra ingredient was love, but Addison was pretty sure it was rum.

"Let me put ice in the glasses then," Addison said as she walked around the breakfast bar.

"Sweetie, why don't you go sit down and let me get everything..."

"Mom, I'm not an invalid," Addison said, getting a little irritated. "In fact, I start my new job in the morning."

"New job?" Adele asked. "Why are you starting a job?"

"Because I'm a grown woman, and I need to work. Sitting around here all day isn't my style," Addison said, cutting her eyes at Jenna and smiling.

"Where will you be working?"

"Jolt."

"What? Rebecca hired you?"

"Yes, and I'm very thankful to have something to do."

"Addy, you really need to stay off your feet. Maybe get an office job. I can call Mrs. Higgins at the temporary agency on West Fourth..." Adele said.

"No! Mom, you can't babysit me for five more months. Pregnant women work all the time. For goodness sakes, you've had five children yourself!" Addison didn't mean to snap at her mother, but she was tired of being treated like she was fragile.

"I just want to make sure you're safe, sweetie. That's all," Adele said, her feelings obviously hurt. Addison walked over to her mother and hugged her.

"I'm sorry, Mom. Pregnancy hormones got the better of me. I'm so thankful for your concern," she whispered.

"You just let me know what you need," Adele said as she pulled back and went back to her fruitcakes. "I just can't wait to meet my new grand baby. I don't know which I want more, a boy or a girl. I suppose as long as its healthy..."

"I'm considering adoption," Addison blurted out, the weight of her secret finally becoming too much to bear.

Adele dropped her spoon and looked at Addison, tears in her eyes and her mouth hanging open. "Addison Rose, you can't be serious!" Out of all of the reactions she had expected from her mother, this wasn't one she had considered. Adele Parker was always the epitome of Southern grace and understanding, and this side of her was something Addison had rarely seen in her life.

"Mom..." Kyle said, rising up and grabbing her hand across the counter. Jenna's face was also shocked, and Addison felt terrible for throwing this information out like she did. She had intended on waiting until after Christmas, but the pressure was too much for her.

"It's okay, Kyle. I shouldn't have said it like that,

without warning. Of course, how do you warn people you're about to say something shocking?" Addison was rambling now, so she slid down onto an empty barstool and took a deep breath.

"Addison, are you sure about this?" Kyle asked.

"No, I'm not. I said I'm considering it, Kyle. I don't know what I want to do yet. I'm keeping my options open, and I'm trying to make sense of this situation. I want to do the right thing for this child. I just don't want anyone getting too attached to this baby because he or she might not be a member of this family in the end." Her words got softer as she reached the end of that sentence.

"That baby is already a member of this family, Addison Rose," Adele said through deep breaths. "That is my grand baby and your child. How can you even consider giving your baby away?"

"Stop, Mom. She has enough pressure on her!" Kyle snapped, and it was completely out of character for him. He'd never raised his voice at his mother like that before, but he'd also never seen her so judgmental about something.

Adele took a deep breath and walked slowly over to Addison. She put her hand on Addison's arm. "I'm sorry, honey. I don't mean to push you. I know this must be very difficult, but you're not thinking clearly. My Addison would never consider giving her own baby to strangers."

Addison looked at her mother and felt more alone than she ever had. "Well, maybe I'm not the Addison you once knew, mother. I'm a grown woman, and this is my decision to make," Addison said as she stood. "I'm a little tired, so I think I'll go lie down for a while."

She walked away from the kitchen and toward the foyer with Kyle calling behind her. But for once in her life, she ignored her brother and just kept walking.

～

ADDISON AWOKE WITH A START. Her heart was pounding and she could see slivers of moonlight peeking through her window. It was now well past dinner, she assumed, as she rolled over and looked at her alarm clock. It read 10:56 PM and her stomach growled.

What kind of mother would she be if she hadn't fed her baby dinner? The negative thoughts about herself had been increasing lately. Jim had really done a number on her psyche since they married, and she'd allowed it so how weak did that make her?

She sat up on the side of her bed and slipped her feet into her fuzzy bunny slippers. Her mom had changed little about her room since she moved out, and those slippers had been her prized possession in high school. Her high school boyfriend, Mike Holland, had given the pink pigs to her for Valentine's Day. Of course, her relationship with Mike lasted only a short time until he realized he was gay and liked Petey Callahan. The thought made Addison giggle to herself.

Making her way downstairs, Addison hoped there would be something left over from dinner rather than fruitcake. She loved her mother, but she'd never developed a taste for her famous fruitcakes which made her an immediate outcast in her family as far as she was concerned.

Maybe she was being too hard on herself and her family. They loved her, and she knew that. Maybe it was pregnancy hormones or something, but she just wanted to yell at everyone about anything. Actually, she wanted to yell at Jim for creating this whole mess in the first place, but what good would that do? She was already getting creamed in divorce court, and now she'd be named a whore too.

Ugh.

"Addison?" she heard her mother's voice say softly. Addison jumped in fright as she turned to see her mother sitting in the darkened kitchen. She was eating a slice of fruitcake and drinking a glass of milk. Her mother never ate at night, and was always in bed by ten so this scene made no sense.

"Mom, you scared the living daylights out of me!" Addison said, holding her hand to her chest.

"I'm sorry, honey. I didn't mean to. I've been doing a lot of things I don't mean to do lately," she said sighing. "I'm sorry about earlier."

Addison adored her mother. If anything, she wanted to be just like her. Strong. Independent. Loyal. "I'm the one who should be saying sorry. I sprung something very big on you like I was ordering a pizza. I should have prepared you and not just blurted it out like that."

"But I should have been more understanding. It's just that I was in shock, and I reacted badly. Here, sit down," Adele said, pushing out the bar stool next to her. Addison took a seat, but she was secretly starving and wishing she'd made it to the refrigerator before she was invited to sit down. "Fruitcake?" Adele asked, offering her a bite.

"No. Thanks," Addison said as she sat down, unable to shatter her mother's dreams that everyone liked her fruitcake.

"I talked to Kyle and Jenna a lot after you went upstairs, and they made me understand that this is your decision. I still look at you as my little girl, Addy, and it's taking everything in me not to find Jim and give him a swift kick in the butt," she said, her lips pursed. Addison smiled and reached over to hold her mother's hand. "Butt" was about the worst word she'd ever heard come out of her mother's mouth.

"I can't say I understand because I'm not a mother, but I respect that. I'm glad you're my mom," she said softly. Adele leaned over and gave her a kiss on the cheek.

"Still, you need to take care of yourself and that baby, so I want you to see the doctor this week. If you don't mind, I'll set an appointment for you."

"That'd be great. Thanks."

"Good. Well, I'm going to hit the sack. I just couldn't sleep," Adele said as she stood up and yawned.

"Maybe your secret ingredient will help you sleep," Addison said softly. Her mother chuckled.

"Maybe."

As Adele made her way to the foyer, Addison called out to her.

"Mom?"

"Yes?" she said, turning around.

"I really appreciate your support, and I haven't made a final decision yet. Anything could happen, right?"

"That's very true," Adele said with a wink before she disappeared in the dark hallway leading to her bedroom.

~

"I STILL DON'T GET why we're taking the ferry to the island this morning. It's freaking cold out here!" Aaron complained to his older brother, Jackson. The brothers and their girlfriends were all standing in the parking lot of the ferry dock, the blustery December wind whipping up around them.

"Because the ladies want to go, and we do what the ladies want to do," Jackson said, laughing as he elbowed his brother in the side.

Both Rebecca and Tessa had insisted on coming out to the island to do some "scouting" for the reception that they planned to hold there after Kyle and Jenna got married in the spring.

The island had become "their" place, and the women thought having the wedding reception there would be perfect. Kyle and Jenna had finally decided to have their wedding right there on the ferry.

"Can't we do this on a warmer day?" Aaron said as his teeth chattered. The skinniest of the Parker brothers had also always been the least tolerable of cold, which was one good reason to live near the beach.

"It's December. What warmer day are you thinking of?" Tessa asked. "Besides, I can keep you warm," she purred as she snuggled into Aaron's chest and kissed his chin.

"Oh, good Lord. Get a room!" Jackson said rolling his eyes.

"Hey, hey, hey!" a voice boomed from the ferry. "Ya'll comin'? I ain't getting any younger over here!" Clay Hampton, an old friend of the Parker kids, ran the local ferry service. As more tourists found out about January Cove, his business was finally getting busier. But Jackson honestly didn't know how Clay made ends meet. His business was seasonal for sure, but even spring and summer didn't bring the huge bunch of tourists that he would have gotten in other areas of coastal Georgia.

"I know you ain't getting any younger!" Aaron called back to him. Clay waved his hand at him in mock offense.

They walked over to the ferry, and the men shook hands. Clay had long been considered one of January Cove's most eligible bachelors. With rugged good looks and crystal clear blue eyes, the women loved him but Clay never seemed fazed by it. Some people in the town even questioned whether he was gay for awhile, but he put that to rest when he dated Samantha Lambert for two years.

Everyone thought they would marry one day, but then the whole thing just seemed to fall apart in the blink of an eye. Clay rarely discussed dating the famous model from Savannah, but at least it cemented his status of being a typical heterosexual male.

"Any other crazy people riding this glorified fishing boat today?" Aaron ribbed as they stepped aboard the small ferry.

"Nope, just you crazies," Clay said as he leaned in and kissed Rebecca and Tessa on their cheeks.

"Quit complaining, sweetie," Tessa urged sweetly.

"You're girlfriend just called you a wimp," Jackson joked.

"That's not what I said!" Tessa said, slapping Jackson playfully on the arm.

"Jackson Parker, don't you get involved in their business," Rebecca said pinching him.

"Hey, hey, hey! No abuse on this boat!" Clay loved to joke around with the Parker siblings.

They had grown up together, attending high school at JCHS at different times. He had played football with Jackson, baseball with Kyle and picked on little Addison. He and Brad had been on the yearbook committee together, and Aaron, the youngest Parker sibling, had even gone camping with his family a couple of times. In essence, Clay Hampton was the fifth Parker brother.

Clay had spent the better part of his high school experience picking at the only female Parker sibling. He was basically another brother to her. Some people thought he was flirting with her as they got older, but her brothers had threatened Clay beyond an inch of his life if he touched a hair on Addison's head. So he'd held back on any advances. And then she was taken - first by her high school boyfriend and then by her husband, Jim. Clay had met him once and wasn't impressed.

"So, what's the reason for the island trip today?" Clay asked as they made their way out of the docking area.

"Well, we're planning the reception out here after Kyle and Jenna get married on the ferry," Tessa said.

"Shouldn't they be here too?"

"Nah. They're allowing us to take control of the reception," Jackson said.

"Yeah, they aren't stupid. They're somewhere warm right now," Aaron said as everyone on the ferry simultaneously told him to shut up.

~

"So, I think this would be the best place to set up the tent," Rebecca said, waving her hand on a flat area of sand shaded by a few trees.

"Tent? What is this? A circus?" Aaron asked.

"Aaron, what's with all the sarcasm today?" Tessa asked as she pecked him on the lips.

"I'm just talented, I suppose," he said, pulling her closer and planting his lips on hers. "Mmm, you taste like apple pie."

"New lip gloss," she said, staring up into his eyes. "You know, one day this might be us."

"What might be us?"

"Planning our wedding reception..."

"Oh really? I don't believe I've proposed, Tessa," he said with a sly smile.

"I have faith in you, Aaron Parker," she said with a giggle.

Aaron and Tessa had been dating only a short time, but he knew in his heart she was the woman for him. He met her while running his RV campground, Crystal Cove, a popular place for area tourists to enjoy January Cove. Tessa had been on the run from her abusive husband, secluding herself in a ramshackle trailer with her young son when Aaron first spotted her.

Still, his heart had been broken by his former girlfriend, Natalie, when she cheated on him. Somewhere, deep in his heart, that betrayal had tainted him in a way he still couldn't explain. He loved Tessa with his whole heart, but he still wondered if she might one day do the same. Of course, he'd never vocalized that to Tessa as it would've broken her heart, he was sure.

"I'm glad you have faith in me," he said, running his hand over the back of her head and down her neck. "But let's not rush things, Tessa. We have the rest of our lives ahead of us."

For a split second, there was a look of confusion on Tessa's face followed by disappointment. But she quickly replaced it with her sweet smile, which left Aaron wondering if he'd said the wrong thing.

"Come on, let's join the others," she said, still smiling sweetly as she pulled out of his grip and walked toward Rebecca and Jackson.

CHAPTER 4

"So, what's been going on around the Parker house these days?" Clay asked as he rested his hand on the steering wheel of the ferry and chatted with Aaron and Jackson.

"Well, Mom is busy decorating for Christmas, of course," Jackson said laughing. "You know how Adele Parker loves her Christmas decorations."

"Of course. And I assume fruitcake is being made by the truck full?" Clay asked, his dimpled grin on full display. Clay could have been a model if he'd wanted, but he was too dang down to Earth to pursue anything that would put him on display.

"And Addison's home," Aaron said. The revelation shocked Clay, and he felt his breath catch in his throat. Addison was home.

The last time he'd seen her was years ago, just after she married Jim. She'd brought him home for Adele's birthday party, and Clay had come by to help hang up the decorations around the Parker house.

Addison had grown into a beautiful woman. She'd grown her hair longer, and her girlish figure had been replaced with womanly curves that had Clay staring at her a little too much. Jackson had caught him looking once and made it abundantly clear that Addison was married and he was to keep his eyes off of her "curves".

"Addison's home? With Jim?" he asked nonchalantly. Jackson and Aaron looked at each other, their eyes darting around for a moment. "What?" It was readily apparent to Clay that something odd was going on.

"Jim and Addison are divorcing," Jackson said. "But don't take that as an invitation." Jackson eyed his friend carefully, a look of warning in his eyes.

"Chill out, Jackson. I'm not planning on making any moves on your sister. It would just be nice to see her again. It's been a few years. And you know, we grew up together too. I'm allowed to care about what happens to her and how she's doing."

"Well, she's going through a lot right now, and I don't want anything upsetting her further. The divorce isn't going well. Jim's a jackass."

"Could've told you that years ago. Never liked that guy. He doesn't deserve her anyway," Clay said.

"She's working at Jolt with me now," Rebecca volunteered as she walked up and wrapped her arms around Jackson's shoulders from behind. "In fact, we did some training early this morning."

"So she's at Jolt now?" Clay asked, still not making eye contact with any of them and instead keeping his eyes on the water. "Maybe I'll stop by for a cup of coffee later..."

"I'm sure she'd love to see you, but she won't be back in until tomorrow morning," Rebecca said, giving Jackson a warning look to keep his mouth shut. It wasn't that Jackson didn't like Clay. He just couldn't stomach the thought of his sister being ogled... by anyone.

It had been very hard to let Addison grow up. Being the only girl, all of the boys had been somewhat protective over her. But Jackson had been like a father to her growing up, and he figured those feelings of protection were never going to change. Jim had already damaged her, and he didn't intend to let anyone else harm her again. Plus, with a baby on the way, Jackson now felt protective over two people.

"Well, nothing starts a day like a cup of coffee," Clay said, winking at Rebecca.

∼

ADDISON HAD NEVER BEEN a morning person, but since being pregnant she seemed to rise earlier and earlier. Maybe it was God's way of preparing her for the long nights of being a new mother. Whatever it was, it was becoming irritating, she thought to herself as she looked at the clock on her nightstand. Six thirty in the morning? The coffee shop opened in an hour, but she didn't need to be there until eight-thirty.

She grabbed a muffin and tossed it into her purse on the way out the door and decided to take a walk on the beach to get her bearings for the day. Addison's mind was full of problems these days. The problem of being pregnant and not knowing what she wanted to do about the baby. The problem of a terrible, contentious divorce. The problem of a floundering career. Everything had seemed so good until it wasn't.

She walked slowly, savoring the smell of the salty sea air. The beach had always been her refuge, even as a kid. So many events had been centered around the beach, from July 4th picnics to family photos to school field trips. She found her center there. Her soul was a mixture of sand and salty water, she was certain of it.

As she made her way down the beach toward the ferry dock, she found a big rock and sat down. Pregnancy was making her more tired than she'd expected. Plus, she had been plagued with unrelenting morning sickness the last couple of days. Everyone said the second trimester was better, but her morning sickness had just begun.

Thankfully, her small frame had allowed her to gain weight slowly so far, and she wasn't showing all that much yet. In fact, Jenna had kidded that she couldn't even tell she was pregnant from behind. Still, she could feel a small pooch starting to form below her belly button, and it wouldn't be long before others could tell too.

She knew it was a matter of time before the whole town would know, and everyone would assume Jim was the father. Yet, Jim was nowhere to be found so she'd be stuck looking like the jilted, pregnant wife. On the other hand, if she told the truth, she'd look like a whore, plain and simple. There was no good answer.

Addison sighed and closed her eyes, taking in the quiet solitude of the ocean. The sound of the waves. The feel of the cold rock under her hands. The smell of coffee? She opened her eyes.

"Clay Hampton?" she said, shocked when she saw her old childhood friend was standing before her, drinking coffee from a thermal mug. What was more shocking than seeing him was how incredibly handsome he was in the early morning light. Or maybe it was pregnancy hormones.

"Hey, Addy," he said with his dimpled smile. She stood slowly, trying to suck her stomach in a bit, and hugged him. He smelled as incredible as he looked, a mixture of salty water and some kind of cologne. And their hug lingered a bit longer than she'd thought it would.

"What are you doing out here so early?" she asked as she sat back down and he joined her on the rock.

"I love getting to the beach early in the morning and watching the sunrise. Helps me focus better during the day," he said, taking another sip of his coffee. "I heard you were back."

"You did?" she said, a little shocked that the town was already finding out she was home.

"Yeah. I saw Jackson and Aaron yesterday. And their ladies," he said, putting air quotes around the word "ladies".

"Ohhh..." she said. "I was probably at Jolt trying to figure out the stupid cash register at the time." Clay laughed, and it was the kind of laugh that's so genuine. Jim never had a genuine laugh. Now, when she thought of him - which she tried to avoid - she imagined him as the Joker from Batman, maniacal laugh and all.

"You doing okay?"

"Why wouldn't I be?"

"Aaron told me about you and Jim. The divorce…"

"I'm going to kill my brother," she said softly, her inner hormonal rage issue creeping to the surface.

"Please don't kill him. We play on the recreational softball league together, and he's a fairly good first baseman. Not the best, but then you take what you can get in January Cove…" he trailed off, his dry humor apparent.

Addison smiled. "Sorry. I'm a little stressed lately. What else did my fabulous brothers tell you?"

"Not much except that Jim is a jackass."

"True story," she said nodding her head.

"Need me to kick his ass?" Clay asked with a wink.

"Maybe. Can I take a rain check on that one?"

"Of course. Seriously, though, if you need to talk to someone… you know, just to vent, if nothing else… I'm here. I know it can be hard talking to family sometimes. They aren't always impartial." She appreciated the sentiment.

"Thanks. I just might take you up on that one day," she said. "Well, I'd better get to Jolt. Don't want to get fired on my first full day. Wish me luck!"

"Good luck, Addy," he said as they both stood. "You'll do fine."

She smiled and started to walk toward the road when he called out to her.

"Hey, Addy?"

"Yeah?" she said, turning to see the sunrise in full force above the ocean, streaks of orange and yellow almost blinding her vision.

"For what it's worth, I always thought Jim was a jackass." He grinned, those dimples making her legs feel a little weak.

"Well, I wish you would've told me!" she said, laughing as she turned and walked toward Jolt.

~

"OKAY, so when you take their order, you just press this button here and then hit total. Take the receipt and give one copy to the customer and then take this copy and put in under the drawer..." Rebecca explained again as Addison's eyes felt like they were crossing. Why was this so hard for her? She'd been a highly successful businesswoman in Atlanta, designing million dollar houses and high rise condos. Now, she was having problems deciphering how to work a simple cash register in a small coffee house in January Cove. My, how things change in a flash.

"I'm sorry, Rebecca. I know I seem like a complete dunce, but I think it's my hormones," she whispered.

"Sweetie, it's no big deal. Trust me. I'm very laid back. You'll catch on," she said, smiling as she held Addison's shoulders. "You know, I came from New York where life is fast paced and hectic. It was an adjustment moving to January Cove, as I'm sure it has been for you coming back from Atlanta."

"Yeah, it's an adjustment for sure. I mean, I grew up here but I've been gone for so long. I really thought I left this place behind." Addison sighed and looked out the large plate glass window facing January Cove's main street. It was a far cry from the sky scrapers of Atlanta.

"Pardon me for asking, but why would you want to leave this place behind, Addy? I mean, your family is here and this town is a jewel. Most people would kill to live in a place like January Cove."

"I know, and I feel bad that I was trying to leave it behind," she said, a sad smile playing on her lips. She leaned against the counter and crossed her arms. "Do you know what it's like to grow up with four brothers?"

"No. I was an only child. I only know what's it's like to grow up lonely."

"Well, it's a double edged sword. On the one hand, you have all of these guys to protect you. But on the other hand, it's hard to live your life when someone is always watching. I could barely date in high school because Jackson would try to interrogate every guy who came along," she said giggling. "Once, this boy I'd been drooling over for months finally asked me out and Jackson scared him so bad that he switched schools!"

"Seriously?" she said laughing. "That Jackson Parker is something else."

"Then I finally had my high school boyfriend, but he turned out to be gay."

"Nice..." she said as she started cleaning the espresso machine.

"Yeah, it did wonders for my self esteem," Addison said with a chuckle. "I guess I just wanted to get away and be myself, not a Parker kid. I wanted to make a name for myself and start my own life, free from the protection of my brothers. But look what that got me," she said with a sigh.

"Addy, you had a great life in Atlanta. You had that big career you wanted, and you made a name for yourself. You shouldn't feel bad about yourself because your rat bastard of a husband cheated on you," she said, a little more anger seeping from her than Addison expected. "Sorry. I just hate cheaters."

Addison realized she was a cheater too. "Rebecca, I'm the one standing here pregnant with another man's baby. Yeah, Jim was wrong for what he did, but I basically did the same thing. I'm still married."

"It's not the same, Addison."

"Why? Because he started it? That would be an immature way of looking at it, wouldn't it?" she asked. Rebecca bit her lips and rubbed Addison's arm.

"I'm so sorry that you're going through all this. But it will get better. Trust me. Even when you're at rock bottom, things always get better."

Addison knew that Rebecca was speaking from experience. After losing her husband in the September 11th bombings in NYC, Rebecca had been left to raise her young son alone. Leo, now almost fifteen years old, didn't remember his father. It occurred to Addison that her baby would never know its father either, whether she gave it up for adoption or not.

Her heart hurt.

What kind of life could she provide for her child as a single mother working in a coffee shop? She didn't want to struggle to make ends meet like her own mother had in those early days, but then again Adele Parker had picked herself up by her bootstraps after the death of her husband and started a thriving real estate business. Addison knew it could be done, but she didn't know if she had the fortitude to do it.

Addison spent the first half of the day learning the ropes at Jolt, everything from how the coffee machines worked to how to make the perfect blueberry scone. It was a far cry from her interior design business, but it was calm and quiet, which was what she needed right now.

Her plan was to stash every dime she made at Jolt, which wasn't much, and save up to get her own place. Maybe it would be in January Cove or maybe somewhere closer to the city again, although she doubted she could afford that.

Adele would want her to stay at the house for as long as possible, and Addison knew that, but she was far too proud to take handouts from anyone, including her mother.

After lunchtime, the coffee shop slowed to a crawl. Rebecca had gone to a parent/teacher meeting at Leo's school and Addison was left twiddling her thumbs. She wiped the tables down twenty times and practiced on the cash register, but she was getting bored.

She stood at the window and stared across the street at the ocean, wishing it was mid summer and she had a bikini body again. Boy, she'd had some fantastic times at that beach with her brothers and mother. Fishing off the pier had been one of her favorite past times with Kyle, and she thought she might just do a little fishing soon to clear her head and reacquaint herself with the sea.

As she was lost in thought, her cell phone rang and she ran to grab it. The number was unknown, so she picked it up in case it was an urgent call about one of her family members.

"Hello?"

"Well, there you are," the familiar voice of her soon-to-be ex husband said. Funny how she used to think his voice was strong and sexy, but now it sounded evil and sickening to her.

She'd been avoiding calls from his cell phone and office numbers for weeks, but he'd finally gotten her to answer. She almost hung up, but morbid curiosity got the best of her.

"What do you want, Jim?" she said, her voice even and full of anger at the same time.

"Don't you think we need to talk, Addy?" he said, adding strong emphasis to her name.

"Don't call me Addy. That's reserved for people who love me."

"I tried to love you, but you made it impossible

when you bedded some guy in a bar and got knocked up. By the way, way to go on that one."

"Jim, if you're calling just to harass me, I'll file a restraining order."

"Whatever. We need to discuss our divorce settlement."

"What settlement? Last time I heard, you were trying to take everything and leave me with nothing."

"You make it sound bad, sweetheart. I just want my fair share, and since your piddly little interior design hobby amounted to squat in terms of our monthly income, I deserve the lion's share of our property and finances."

"Well, that's not how my attorney sees it." She was growing weary of this conversation and was sorry she'd answered the phone. Next time she saw an unknown number, she wasn't picking it up. She walked behind the counter and leaned against it, staring at the coffee pot as a distraction.

"Your attorney? Are you talking about that schmuck, Helen Monroe? Wow, Addison, you're really out of touch. First of all, she's as old as homemade sin and hasn't won a case in four years. Everyone knows she's just waiting for death at this point," he said, chuckling into the phone like the Joker she thought of him as these days.

He was probably right about old Helen. Addison hadn't been able to afford a top notch attorney, which Jim knew all too well. Plus, he was so well connected in Atlanta that no one would've taken her case anyway for fear of retribution. Jim wielded a lot of power in the legal community.

"Jim, I'm busy right now. Just get to the point."

"The point is that you need to face facts. You're not getting anything, and you're just wasting precious money that you don't have fighting me on this. You're not dealing with an amateur, Addison. I'll destroy you, and you know it, so why not save yourself money and time and sign the agreement?"

A rage she'd never felt in her life welled up inside of her. Her hands shook and sweat started beading on her forehead. This kind of stress couldn't be good for the baby or her.

"Let me tell you something, Jimbo," she said, sure that would irritate him as he hated his old nickname, "There isn't a snowball's chance in hell that I'm going to let you take me to the cleaners. I'll fight you until my last breath because you didn't build that business of yours without my help. So, you just dig your heels in, buddy boy, because we're about to have a showdown. You hear me?"

"You're a stupid, stupid woman."

"Kiss my ass, Jim!" she said as she pressed the end button on her phone and slammed it onto the counter, cracking the screen in the process. When she saw the screen, she burst into tears. Just add that to the list of broken parts of her life.

"Addy, you okay?" she heard Clay say behind her. She was so embarrassed.

"What? Yeah. I'm fine," she said, wiping the tears from her cheeks with the back of her hand. "What can I get for you?" she said, holding onto the sides of the cash register for dear life.

Clay stepped toward and pried her hands from the cash register, pulling her around the counter and into a chair. "You're not okay. What's going on?"

In that moment, she was so thankful for the ruffly apron she was wearing. Any day now, people were going to get suspicious about her belly enlarging.

"It was Jim. On the phone."

"Ah…. I heard you say someone needed to kiss your ass. Thought it might be an open invitation."

Addison burst into laughter, the tears falling from her eyes at the same time. "You're a nut!" she said, wiping her eyes. "Thanks. I needed some comic relief. I swear Rebecca's going to want to fire me if I don't get it together."

"I doubt that. She's practically a Parker family member already. Plus, Adele would knock her out for firing the prodigal daughter."

"Probably," Addison said. "Seriously, can I get you something?"

"Nah. I was just walking by on my way home. Thought I'd say hello. Again."

Something in the way he said it gave her butterflies in her stomach. But she couldn't be getting interested in anyone right now, let alone the guy she thought of as a brother growing up. Still, he *was* looking extremely hot these days.

"I heard you live down off Cherry Street?"

"Yep. Couple doors down from my parents."

"How are they doing?"

"Fairly good. Dad's got some early dementia, but Mom's still spry as she ever was."

Addison smiled. "I loved your Mom. She made the best blueberry pancakes!"

"Still does! You'll have to come say hello while you're in town. She'd love to see you," Clay said.

"Maybe I'll do that one day soon," Addison replied.

"Well, I'd better get home for lunch. Good to see you again, Addy. And don't let Jim get you down, okay?" he said as he rose from his chair. Addison stood as well.

"Easier said than done, I'm afraid," she said.

"He's not worth it, Addy. Even if you walk away with nothing, you're still better off without that jerk. You deserve so much more," he said, seeming to stop himself from saying more.

"Thanks, but you're biased. You're practically a brother to me, Clay," she said with a smile.

"A brother. Hmm, I guess I can see why you'd think that." Again, an odd response. She didn't have the brainpower to think about it in depth. "See ya later," he said as he smiled and waved before disappearing outside.

CHAPTER 5

*A*s soon as Addison opened the front door, she knew she was going to be sick. Her mother was cooking fish, and that was one of her morning sickness "no-no" foods. The list was ever-growing, like her waistline, but fish was high on that list. Just the smell sent her running for the nearest bathroom, often just gagging continuously and never actually throwing up. The dry heaves were almost worse than real throwing up. How was she so lucky to get morning sickness in her second trimester?

Adele called from the kitchen as Addison closed the front door behind her, hand over her mouth as if that would keep her from starting the whole process.

"Hello, dear!" Adele called as Addison rushed through the foyer and into the powder room. Crouched over the rarely used toilet with her feet pushed into the base of the pedestal sink, she was at her lowest of lows. "Addison, are you okay?" her mother asked from behind her.

"Morning sickness, mother. That's all," Addison squeaked out in between dry heaves.

"Oh, dear, is it the fish smell?" Adele asked, suddenly aware of what she had done.

"Mhmmm…" Addison mumbled, trying not to open her mouth. "I'm sorry, Mom, but I have to get outside in the fresh air," she said as she jumped up and ran back out the front door. Sitting on the stoop, she put her head in her hands as she worked to stop the cold sweats she was having. The dry heaving stopped, but her stomach was still churning when her mother came outside followed by Jenna and Tessa.

"Oh, I remember those days very well," Jenna said. "I had horrible morning sickness with Kaitlyn. I swore that child was a demon trying to escape my body!"

"I don't know why I'm suddenly having morning sickness four months in, but I guess that's why I'm not gaining a lot of weight yet," Addison said, wiping her brow with a warm, wet washcloth her mother brought outside.

"I've made an appointment with Dr. Sylvan for tomorrow morning. Maybe she can help you with some remedies," Adele said.

"The best thing that worked for me was ginger. Anything with ginger. Ginger ale. Ginger salad dressing…" Tessa said. Addison started gagging again.

"Please, no more food talk right now…"

"Sorry," Tessa said, feeling bad that she'd said anything. "Is there anything we can do?"

Addison got her bearings once again and surveyed the amazing women sitting beside her. Two weren't officially family to her yet, but she considered them to be already.

"No, but thanks. Mom, I think I'll just go up to my room and lie down for awhile."

Adele looked remorseful. "Honey, I'm so sorry. I will air out the house for a few hours, I promise. And spray air freshener…"

"No air freshener please. That might do more harm than good," Addison said wearily.

"Okay. No air freshener then."

Addison felt terrible for putting everybody out in more ways than one. Here she was sounding ungrateful for the dinner her mother had cooked. Fish had always been one of her favorites, but pregnancy had stolen her taste for it at the moment.

She slowly stood, put her hand over her nose and walked inside and up the stairs. Thankfully, the smell hadn't made its way upstairs yet, so she was able to close her door and get a reprieve from the noxious odor that was assaulting her senses moments before.

She shrugged out of her work clothes, which themselves smelled like a mixture of coffee and blueberry scones, and tossed them into the hamper beside her closet. She then ran a hot bubble bath and spent the next half hour soaking before she fell into her bed and into a blissful sleep.

~

SOMEHOW, Addison had slept right through dinner yet again. Pregnancy was greatly affecting her ability to act normally these days. When she walked downstairs that morning, she wasn't at all surprised to see her mother standing there, purse in hand, waiting for her.

"Addy, your appointment is in twenty minutes, sweetie," she said, smiling through somewhat gritted teeth.

"Oh, gosh, I totally forgot..." Addison said, still wiping the sleep from her eyes. "I slept right through dinner last night. I need to grab a bite and get ready."

"Well, hurry along because we can't keep Dr. Sylvan waiting," Adele chided. No matter how old Addison was, her mother was still her mother. Prompt. Put together. Stern. Independent.

And she wondered if she could ever measure up to be that kind of mother.

Fifteen minutes later, Addison and her mother were turning the corner onto the road where Dr. Sylvan's office was located. A small, white cottage style building right off Main Street housed the popular OBGYN's office. They pulled into the parking lot and walked toward the building.

"Dr. Sylvan is a very good client of mine, you know," Adele said.

"I remember. Didn't you sell her this building a few years ago?"

"I did. But that's not why I mention it," Adele said, stopping just short of the door and looking at Addison.

"Oh... I get it. You don't want her to know about my situation?" Addison said, feeling a little defeated. Adele's eyes got wide.

"Of course not, Addy! I've already told you that

we're proud of you and the woman you've become. I'm not ashamed of this situation at all. What I meant to say is that I know you don't want it spread around town just yet, and Dr. Sylvan is bound by doctor patient confidentiality, so you can tell her anything. Okay?" Adele said, pushing a stray hair off Addison's forehead.

"Thanks, Mom. I appreciate all the support. I really do," she said softly.

An hour later, Addison and her mother were getting back in the car. She had loved Dr. Sylvan and felt good that she now had a doctor monitoring her care. The baby's heartbeat was strong, and her blood pressure and vital signs all looked good. She would get her first ultrasound in a couple of weeks and maybe even find out the sex of the baby.

The pregnancy was becoming more real everyday. No longer could she try to pretend everything was normal in her world. Soon, everyone would know she was pregnant and getting divorced, and eventually the info about it not being her husband's baby would be public knowledge too.

"You know," Adele said as she drove, "I was thinking about turning Brad's old room into a nursery for the baby." She didn't make eye contact with Addison, and she knew it was because her mother was sweetly digging for information on whether Addison had made a decision on adoption yet.

"Mom…"

"I'm not trying to push, sweetie. It was just an idea. Brad's room has that lovely built in bookcase which would be great for a nursery. Plus, it faces the garden out back."

"I know, but there won't be a need for a nursery if I decide on adoption, Mom."

Adele pulled off the side of the road and looked at her daughter. "Addison Rose, I'm your mother. I know you better than anyone else on Earth, and I don't think you're convinced at all on this whole adoption idea."

"I'm not convinced, Mom, but I already told you that I haven't made up my mind totally. There's a lot to think about," she said, staring out into the vast ocean.

"Maybe I can help you consider the options…"

"I appreciate it. I really do. But this is kind of a personal decision, and you're not exactly the most objective about this," Addison said with a smile. "I already know where you stand."

"That's true, but I don't think you really understand why I feel the way I do."

"What do you mean?"

"Nobody knows this, but your aunt Susan gave up a baby when she was nineteen years old," Adele said, referring to her younger sister. Susan lived in Virginia now, and Addison hadn't seen her in years.

"Really?"

"Yes. It was an embarrassing situation for our parents. Back then, girls were sent away to special homes if they got pregnant out of wedlock. Susan wasn't given the choice of putting her baby up for adoption. That was decided for her, mainly by society. Anyway, she went away to the girl's home, which was at a convent up north, and then she came back after having the baby. Susan was never the same again. She became despondent and tried to take her life a couple of times during her twenties. Then she met Arthur, her husband, and things got better. But even now, she brings her baby up on occasion when we talk. She still cries and wonders where her baby girl ended up, what kind of life she had, if she's still alive..."

"Wow, I had no idea."

"I know there are women who give up babies all the time and go on to have full lives, but I also know that there must be a hole in their hearts because once you're a mother, you're always a mother, Addy. That pain is real, and it will always be with you. Just like you miss your Daddy, your child will feel the absence of you too. It's unavoidable. I just want you to think through everything before making a rash decision, and then I will support you no matter what. But you have to ask yourself if you can deal with not knowing your baby."

"I would opt for an open adoption so I could still have access..."

"Addy, how hard will that be, though? Watching someone raise your child? Only seeing pictures? Won't that make the wound even worse?"

"Mom, you're not helping here," she said, getting irritated.

"I'm sorry, but I'm your mother and I want to be honest with you. I just don't think you're going to be okay with this. I know you. I know you have a heart of gold, and inside I think you want to raise this baby, but you don't want people to judge you."

"It's not that, Mom," she said, tears starting to well

in her eyes. "I'm not sure I want to raise this baby because I don't know if I'm enough. All this baby will have is me. I'm about to be divorced, my career is in the tank and I'm living with my mother. That's not enough for a baby."

"Honey, this phase of your life is temporary. Things will get better. I just don't want you to make a permanent decision based on temporary circumstances."

Addison reached for the door handle and cracked the door. "I need to clear my head," she said stepping out.

"Addy, honey, wait…"

"I'm okay. Really. I just need some time. I think I'll take a walk on the beach," she said, wrapping her sweater around her.

"I'm sorry. I didn't mean to upset you again…" Adele said as Addison shut the door and looked into the now open window.

"You brought up some valid points. Now I need to think about them. I'll see you a little later," she said with a weary smile before walking down the path to the beach.

~

IT WAS GETTING COLDER in January Cove by the day, and Addison was having a hard time adjusting for some reason. Right now, she wanted to be somewhere warm and cozy, maybe a tropical island where no one knew her.

Deep down, she realized that she was becoming a

bit of a whiny baby and she hated that trait in other people. Addison had always been the renegade of the Parker family, always going her own way. Now, she felt like curling up in the corner in a fetal position and waiting for nine months to pass.

Her mother was right about one thing. She was nowhere near prepared to hand her baby over to a stranger. It wasn't that she had any problem with adoption per se. In fact, she'd love to adopt a child herself. One day. Maybe.

Giving up her own flesh and blood seemed impossible. But didn't hard decisions always seem impossible anyway?

Still, she felt too conflicted to make a decision just yet. After all, this wasn't a decision to be made overnight.

She pulled her sweater around her tighter and walked toward the ferry. Maybe she'd take a quick run to the island to clear her head. The last time she'd ridden the ferry was ages ago when old Mr. Denton used to make the daily run. Now that January Cove was more popular, she hoped that the ferry wasn't full this time of year because she really just wanted to be alone.

"And we meet again?" she heard a voice say from behind the ferry. There was Clay... again. Was he following her?

"Clay... Are you taking a ride too?"

He smiled, and those memorable dimples reappeared. She remembered being a young girl and practically drooling over the handsome Clay Hampton. He was everything any red blooded American Southern girl would want. Tall, dark, handsome, dimples, tight butt.... Wait, her hormones were getting the better of her again.

"Um, Addy, I run the ferry service." She felt really stupid now.

"See? This is why I should've subscribed to the The Cove Chronicle. I'm so behind on my local news," she said laughing while simultaneously blushing. How could she be so cold and so hot at the same time?

"Going to the island? In this cold? And this early in the morning? That's not the Addison Parker I remember."

"Well, people change, Clay." She didn't mean to sound snide, but it probably came off that way. His smile lingered.

"Come on aboard, ma'am," he said, reaching his hand out to help her onto the ferry. She paused for a moment, looking up into his handsome face, and realized just how honest and trustworthy Clay seemed. Of course, she'd thought the same about Jim when she met him and look how that turned out.

"Am I the only passenger?" she asked, looking around.

"My one and only," he said, and a shiver went up her spine. She kind of liked the sound of being someone's "one and only", but not in the sense that Clay meant at the moment. She'd thought she was Jim's one and only, but apparently it was her, Jim and Tiffani with an "i"... and who knew who else?

"Wow. I expected more people on here this morning."

"Not many people go to the island during this time of the year."

"Then why still run the ferry?" she asked as she stepped aboard and took a seat on one of the built-in benches.

"Because if even one person needs to get to the island, I want to be here to do it." He smiled as he began to back the ferry out of the dock.

"But doesn't it cost more money than you make to cart one person?" she asked, her nosiness getting the best of her.

"It does, but this sea water runs through my veins and I enjoy being the captain of this ferry," he said. "So what brings you here this morning, Addy?" He cocked his head at her with a smile, his beautiful blue eyes staring at her in a way that made her a little bit uncomfortable and comfortable at the same time.

"Just needed some space. And time to think. I've got some decisions to make…"

"Divorce tends to create a lot of decisions that need to be made."

"Yeah…" she said, toying with the idea of telling him about her pregnancy, but her fear got the better of her.

"I'm sorry Jim's giving you such a hard time. If you need any help…"

"I appreciate the offer," she said laughing. "But I've got four brothers who'd be sorely disappointed if I let you kill Jim and not them." Clay let out a huge laugh and nodded his head.

"Very true. But maybe I can be backup just in case one of them is too much of a sissy to finish the job." Addison laughed at that. Clay had always been the one person who could push her brothers' buttons. Male rivalry for sure.

Clay's cell phone rang. He looked down and smiled. "It's my Dad. I'd better take this. He gets confused…"

"Oh, please take it. Don't let me interfere. I'm going to sit back here and clear my mind for awhile," she called as she stood and walked to the back of the ferry. Clay nodded and answered his phone.

"Hi, Dad…"

CHAPTER 6

Staring out into the water, Addison pondered her situation. On the one hand, she wanted to make sure she gave her baby the best life possible. And wouldn't that be with another family that had a mom and a dad who would care for him or her? Wasn't she being selfish to think that she could do both jobs?

Maybe she didn't need to do both jobs. After all, her mother had been a widow for most of Addison's growing up years and had done just fine. Why couldn't Addison be as sure of herself?

Of course, her mother hadn't had a choice. And if she had been in Addison's situation, what choice would she have made? The situations were very different, like apples and oranges.

As the cold wind whipped her face, she felt the familiar sting of warm tears rolling down her cheeks. One thing was for sure, she had to make a decision soon because the stress was doing more harm than good for her and the baby. And if she only got one act as a mother, she wanted to protect her baby from that kind of stress.

"You okay?" Clay asked. He was standing behind her, and she hadn't even noticed when they docked at the island.

"What? Oh. Yeah. I'm fine," she said, quickly wiping a stray tear off her cheek. "You must think I'm a sissy just like my brothers."

"I don't think you're a sissy," he said, sitting down beside her on the bench seat. "In fact, I think you've got more courage in your little finger than most people have in their whole bodies."

"Really?" she asked, a look of surprise apparent on her face.

"Absolutely. I remember when Jackson told me you were taking off to Atlanta to pursue your dream of being an interior designer. That took guts to leave January Cove and your whole family."

"A lot of people do stuff like that, Clay," she said smiling. "Again, I think you're a bit biased."

"It took courage, Addy, and you still have that same courage."

"How do ya figure that? I've been crying since I got here!"

"Because you left Atlanta and your marriage when you realized that Jim was the scum of the Earth. You didn't stay and live in misery. You did the harder thing and came back here to start all over. That takes courage too."

"Thanks, but I sure don't feel courageous right now." She sighed and stared at him for a moment. "Can

I ask you something?"

"Sure."

"Why did you stay in January Cove all these years? I mean, I remember what a smart guy you were in school. You could've easily gone to college and had a jet set lifestyle. You were always bigger than this town."

He chuckled. "Just because you *can* do something doesn't mean you *should*."

"You lost me," she said, secretly blaming her pregnancy hormones again.

"I remember that you were a great singer when we did karaoke at the fall festival and yet you didn't pursue singing. Why?" he asked.

"Because it wasn't the right thing for me. Singing doesn't light me up inside like decorating does."

"Well, the same thing can be said for me, I suppose. I could've gotten my business degree and run some big company, but that doesn't float my boat, so to speak," he said with a smile, obviously enjoying his pun. "I always wanted to be a ferry boat captain. I never want to live somewhere that I can't feel the ocean breeze or have the salt water clinging to my skin. I'm happy in January Cove, and I've come to accept that it's okay not to desire some busy life in a city just because I might make more money."

What a refreshing viewpoint, she thought. Jim was always chasing the almighty dollar, no matter what. He had to have the best cars, the biggest TV, the latest electronic gadget. Addison had never cared about that kind of stuff, but it was the world she lived in so she accepted it. She cared more about her mother's peach preserves and how she missed them. She cared about finding the best fabric for her latest upholstery project. She cared about using her artistic talent to decorate a room that filled people with joy in their own homes.

"It's great that you know who you are," she said. "I feel like I've lost myself over the last few years. I don't know who I am anymore. I can't make simple decisions for myself because Jim always made our decisions. I feel a bit lost in my own mind." That was the most honest she'd been in a long time. Clay was just easy to talk to.

"Addy, you're still in there. You just have to strip away what everyone else wants and decide what *you* want. I don't know what kind of decisions you're struggling with, but you'll make the right choice because I know you'll make it with love."

As soon as he said it, she knew.

She knew without a doubt that she was keeping her baby no matter what. She loved her baby already, and that love would be enough to sustain them both.

Her heart smiled. She was scared, for sure, but she took a deep breath. A sigh of relief.

"Thank you."

"I didn't do anything..." he said looking at her with confusion.

"You just did more than you know," she said as she leaned across the seat and hugged him. He was so warm, and it felt good to be in the arms of a caring man for once in her life. She almost didn't want to let go, but this was Clay. He was like a brother to her and she was letting her feelings get clouded.

She pulled back and promptly blushed. Dang Scottish heritage.

"So, tell me about your family," she said, changing the subject.

"Well, I already told you about Mom and Dad. My sister, Amy, lives just outside of Nashville now."

"Wow, Amy moved? That's surprising. I thought she'd never leave January Cove!"

"Well, her choices were limited here. Amy has a degree in music, so she needed to be close to the music scene. She's the mother of a three year old too."

"Really? I didn't even know she was married!" Addy said. By the look on his face, she knew she'd said something wrong.

"Amy's never been married. She wanted a child and chose to have one out of wedlock. The guy's never been involved. Doesn't want to be."

"And how do you feel about that?" Addison asked, bracing herself for the onslaught of judgement he was sure to have about such a decision to have a baby outside of marriage.

"I think my sister is a strong woman and a fantastic mother. I adore my nephew, and I wouldn't have had it any other way. A single mother has to be a tough cookie, and I respect her for it."

Addison literally wanted to kiss him right now. He was amazing. How had she never seen that?

"So, you want to take a walk?" he asked, pointing to the island.

"Sure."

As they walked, Addison caught up on all of the

gossip of January Cove. Clay talked about his father's progressive illness and his mother taking care of him. It was good to catch up with someone who had no agenda. She talked about Jim and what he'd done, about their life together and the loneliness. He was a good listener, and she felt a lot better after their talk.

"Hey, what's that sign over there?" she asked, pointing back to January Cove's main coast that she could see off in the distance.

"Oh, that's the old Mallory plantation house. It's up for sale."

"Really? Gosh, I always loved that place. Remember when we had the cotillions there? All those girls dressed in beautiful dresses. Thank God my mother never made me go," she said laughing.

"It's a beautiful place, but Mr. Mallory passed a few years ago and his estate is finally selling it off. It'd make a great bed and breakfast."

"You're right. January Cove needs another B&B, especially right here in town."

"It needs some work, but it could be restored to something beautiful," he said. "I've never told anyone this, but I've thought a few times about buying it myself and restoring it."

"So that must mean you're really good with your hands?"

"Excuse me?" he said, his eyes as wide as saucers.

"Oh, gosh, I didn't mean…" she said, cackling with laughter. "That didn't sound good, did it?"

"No, it sounded just fine to me…" he stammered.

"Can we change the subject?" Her face burned with embarrassment.

"To answer your question, yes. I am good with my hands," he said with a wink. She blushed even more. "I've done contractor work for years on the side."

Addison smiled when he let her off the hook with the contractor statement. "I would love to decorate that place. Can you imagine what it looked like inside during Christmas back in its heyday? I bet it was gorgeous. I can see fires roaring in the fireplaces and Christmas china on the dining room table..." she closed her eyes and thought of the possibilities. Except she was a broke soon-to-be single mother and not anywhere near owning a B&B. "Oh well. Maybe one day," she said softly into the wind. "Can I ask you something?"

"Of course."

"How in the world would you be able to buy a place like that? I mean, the ferry business is a little...."

"Slow?" he asked with a chuckle.

"Yeah."

"Can I tell you a little secret?"

Addison leaned in like they were surrounded by a crowd. "I love secrets."

"The ferry business is just a hobby for me. It's not where I get my income. I just let everyone think that." Clay's eyes twinkled as he told her his secret.

"Seriously? What do you do then?"

"I'd tell you, but I'd have to kill you." His face went serious for a moment, and she considered the fact that she was on an isolated island with him. Then he started laughing. "Good Lord, you looked terrified for a second!"

"I was just acting!" she said, slapping him on the arm playfully.

"Sure... But seriously, I have some Internet businesses I started a few years ago. A few retail websites and such. That provides my income, and the ferry stuff is just for fun since my sites run themselves most days."

"Why don't you tell anyone?"

"I guess I'm just a private person. I like my anonymity. Besides, when you tell people you work online, they always assume a couple of things. For one, they think it's easy and want me to teach them everything that it took me years to learn. Secondly, they think I must work in porn because that's the only way to make income on the Internet," he said laughing.

"Do you?" she asked giggling.

"Maybe. And I might be hiring for a new female lead..." he said looking her up and down. Addison wanted to slip her enlarging belly out for his review, but decided to keep her secret at the risk of not getting a laugh for once.

"Well, I'm glad you have such a thriving business, Clay. Really. You deserve it."

"Thanks."

"Why haven't you ever found a Mrs. Hampton?" she asked as they walked back toward the ferry.

"I was engaged once, but she wasn't my type at all. A model."

"Oh yeah. I remember that. Jackson showed me her picture once. Samantha?"

"Yeah." He was quiet for a few moments. "And there hasn't been anyone else who can meet the demands of a busy ferry captain, I guess." His face looked a little distant. A little sad. And that made her sad.

Clay deserved someone fantastic by his side. He was a man's man with a soft heart. He'd always been the type that would do anything for anybody, constantly coming to the rescue of people all over town. When they'd had a flash flood once, he spent the day pulling people out of dangerous situations in his truck. When a hurricane hit one year, he'd gone all over town helping people board up their windows, including the Parkers.

He was funny and handsome, but there was a lot more to Clay than met the eye. He had an old soul, but Addison never could figure out what kept him from finding love for himself. Now in his 30's, she would've bet that he'd have been married with kids by now, but here he was captaining a small ferry boat with one passenger. Seemed like a waste.

They climbed aboard the ferry and Clay took his spot at the helm. "Hey, you want to steer this thing?"

"Me? I'm not even a good driver of cars, and you want me to steer the ferry? You must not hold this vessel in high regard, Captain." She pulled her sweater tighter around her and tied it with the belt to avoid if blowing open in the ocean breeze.

"I trust you," was all he said. Her stomach felt like it had butterflies flying around inside of it. Why did that keep happening to her? She decided it was hunger. Yes, pregnant women were hungry, and that must be what was going on.

"Okay, but don't say I didn't warn you," she said as she walked up to the large steering wheel. The ferry was old, no doubt about it. It didn't have the technological advances newer boats would have, but it had history. And Clay seemed to be big on history and tradition.

"You've got to come closer," he said, pulling her in front of him and reaching his arms around her body as he placed her hands on the steering wheel. All of the sudden, she was very aware of his presence. No longer did he feel like "brother Clay", but like a man. A warm, handsome, kind-hearted man that had her in his arms. Or at least had his arms around her. She could feel the strength of his chest pressed against her back, a strong, steady force holding her up. She could feel the warmth of his skin seeping through his shirt, and every part of her suddenly wanted to turn around and put her head on his chest. Weird.

Maybe she was reading too much into the moment, but it felt good. And that made her feel bad. She wasn't the right woman for Clay. Her baggage was too heavy to carry, and she wasn't going to involve someone like him. He deserved the best, and she wasn't it anymore.

"You know what? Why don't you drive so I can sight see?" she said, ducking under his left arm and smiling.

"You grew up here, Addy. What kind of sight seeing do you need to do?" he asked, his face serious. He knew she had moved away for a reason. "Look, I hope I didn't make you feel uncomfortable. I was just trying to show you…"

"No, of course not! I just don't want to drive this heap of metal, that's all," she said, waving her hands at him and trying valiantly to make a joke. There was a reason she wasn't a comedian.

The rest of the trip was almost silent. Clay drove and she sat and stared off into the distance. The last thing she needed right now was more feelings. She already had plenty of feelings about Jim and her marriage and her baby and her career... She didn't need feelings for Clay.

And yet there they were.

CHAPTER 7

The next morning, Addison awoke with renewed hope. She'd made the decision to keep the baby, and that had taken a weight off her shoulders, at least somewhat. But today something else was on her mind and had kept her awake for much of the night.

The bed and breakfast.

Just the mention of it made her very soul feel giddy. She hadn't known that the thought of running a B&B would excite her, and maybe it was more the decorating of the old place that excited her. Even though the idea was completely out of reach financially, she loved dreaming about it. Overnight, she'd decided that she would approach whoever bought it and see if they might let her submit a bid for decorating it.

Maybe things would fall into place. She'd get her divorce, have her baby and start her life over completely. It wouldn't be easy, but it'd be worth it.

As she rolled out of bed, she could feel the difference in her body immediately. The baby was starting to move more, and she could finally feel the flutters of activity in there. Her stomach was tightening over the growing baby bump, and she knew her time hiding it was limited.

"Good morning, baby," she whispered for the first time. She hadn't dared talk to the baby yet for fear she'd grow attached to it and not be able to let it go. But now that fear was gone, and she wanted to bond with that precious life growing inside of her as early as possible. She thought for a moment about the baby's father, Eric, and wondered how he could not care about his child. She had greatly overestimated his character.

When she thought about her own father and what he'd missed out on raising his kids, it was hard to imagine a father willingly giving that relationship up. But she knew that fathers - and mothers - made that choice everyday all across the world. Still, it was a sad choice to make.

"I'm your momma," she continued whispering to the baby as she sat on the side of her bed. "We're going to have lots of fun together. I want you to know I'm going to do my best to be a good mother and teach you everything you need to know in this world. I had a big family, and you're going to have lots of cool uncles who want to take care of you and protect you. And maybe one day you'll even have a brother or sister."

She hoped that was true. That some man out there would love her and she'd love him, and he could be trusted with her heart. And that he'd have such a big heart that he could love someone else's child and protect them with his life. Maybe it was a fairy tale, but she was still holding out hope that men like that existed out there. Somewhere.

She was broken out of her conversation with the baby by her ringing cell phone. It was early in the morning for anyone who really knew her to call, so she ran across the room to grab it before it woke anyone else in the house up.

"Hello?"

"Addison? It's Helen," she heard her attorney say. The woman was as old as dirt with wrinkles that seemed so deep they might show her bones underneath soon. She smoked like a freight train, and her gravelly voice was impossible to miss.

"Oh, hi, Helen. Something wrong?" Addison asked, her stomach already knotting up.

"You might wanna sit down for this one," she said, stopping mid sentence for a cough and then what sounded like a drag of her cigarette. Addison was starting to regret investing what little money she had into this woman. Hasty decisions end up making situations like this worse.

Addison sat down in the chair beside her dresser. "Okay, I'm sitting."

"I'll just cut right to the chase. Jim's attorneys have drawn up papers where Jim gets everything. The house. The bank accounts. The cars."

"How is that possible?"

"Well, he's claiming you didn't deny your infidelity and there's nothing proving he was ever unfaithful to you. You got any text messages or emails or anything showing his affair?"

"No. We always talked in person... or argued, rather. Sometimes we had phone conversations, but Jim hates to text and he never emailed me. He was careful, Helen. He's a freaking attorney. No offense."

"None taken. And I agree. He's a rat bastard. But he's a rat bastard with a lot of power around here, and he's throwing it around something fierce right now."

"Shouldn't I automatically get half of everything?"

"No. Georgia isn't a community property state. We have something called equitable distribution. That means anything bought or earned during the marriage is supposed to be distributed equitably. But, here's the issue. Jim knows you have limited funds right now, and he knows you don't want to spend your whole pregnancy fighting. He's going to use that to either drag this out or force your hand."

"This isn't fair..."

"No, it's not. But his plan, from what I've heard through the grapevine, is reveal your infidelity, your pregnancy, the whole thing. Ruin your career and reputation. So, sweetie, in the end you might get your used car back and a few thousand bucks that he hasn't hidden yet, but you'll be screwed as far as your career and reputation."

Addison couldn't catch her breath. She leaned over, as far as she could anyway, and stuck her head between her knees. She could hear Helen calling her name, but honestly she blacked out for a few moments as her whole life flashed before her eyes. How could she ever start over with nothing? It wasn't fair! She'd contributed a lot to their home and finances, and now she was just supposed to walk away with nothing at all?

"Addison? You there?" Helen called once more. Addison regained her senses for a moment.

"Yeah. Sorry…"

"I've also put together some information on adoption like you asked…"

"No need, Helen. I'm not giving my baby up for adoption. I'm going to raise my baby." A shocked gasp came from somewhere else in the room, and she turned to see her mother standing in the doorway with her hand over her mouth and stifling a huge smile. She gave Addison a thumbs up.

Addison said her goodbyes to Helen and hung up her phone. Adele walked silently across the room and hugged her daughter tight.

"It's going to be okay. You made the right decision, Addy," she whispered into Addison's thick brown hair.

"I sure hope so, because I'm starting over with nothing. Literally. This whole divorce thing couldn't be worse," she said. She explained the whole phone call, and Adele's face showed the anger brewing underneath. She didn't want to cause her mother's blood pressure to go up, so she tried to act nonchalant about it.

"Sweetie, you're strong. You're going to get through this and be better than ever. The Parker women always come out on top, you hear me?" her mother said, grabbing her by the shoulders and looking her in the eyes.

"I hear you," Addison said smiling. "And maybe one day soon I'll believe you."

～

AFTER EXCUSING herself and telling her mother she needed some exercise, Addison found herself walking around the downtown January Cove area before going to work at Jolt. Memories of her formative years flooded her mind as she walked the streets.

The corner drug store, Rudy's, was a mainstay in January Cove. The original owner, Rudy Hilliard, had long since died and the shop had stayed in the family. His grandson, Michael, now owned the place and still ran it in much the same way his forefathers did. There was still a working soda fountain inside, and the decor swept you back to the 1950s. Addison waved at Michael through the window as she walked by, being sure to secure her sweatshirt around her waistline.

Next was JCHS - January Cove High School - and she had many fond memories of that place. Too many to mention. Homecoming dances and proms. Yearbook committee and football games. She adored her years at JCHS, and she longed for those simpler times when the idea of bills and babies and divorce were foreign to her.

As she walked, she saw the ice cream parlor and the dry cleaners and the antique stores that littered the main street through town. And then she passed the old Mallory house.

Seeing it up close made her heart skip a beat. This place held memories for many grown up kids in

January Cove. All those dances and cotillions and weddings. It had been a beautiful place in its time, and now it was a shell of its former self. Kind of like Addison. The irony wasn't lost on her.

The for sale sign was still in the yard, and the place appeared empty. Addison walked slowly up to the front porch and peeked through the windows. It definitely needed some work, but the "bones" were good.

There were flyers on the porch, so she grabbed one and almost passed out when she saw the price. Even with a hefty divorce settlement, she wouldn't come anywhere close to the purchase price. And now she wouldn't be getting a settlement from what she could tell.

She put the flyer back in the box and sank down onto the front step. This was as close as she was ever getting to owning the Mallory house. She felt like such a failure. She was starting her life over again, but this time it was like she was a knocked up teenager with no career aspirations.

She stood and looked through the windows once more. Why was it that she could so vividly imagine herself living there, dancing around one of the four fireplaces with her child while putting up the Christmas tree? There was no way it was ever going to happen. Sometimes fairy tales just don't come true.

"Are you trespassing, ma'am?" a voice said from behind her. It startled her so that she jumped back and fell over an empty flower pot and directly into the man's arms. When she looked up, she realized it was Clay. "Addy, I'm sorry! Are you okay?"

She glared up at him and struggled to get her footing, being careful to pull her sweatshirt down over her belly. "Jeez, Clay! Were you trying to give me a heart attack?"

He started laughing so hard that tears were welling in his eyes. "I thought you knew it was me…"

"Why would I know it was you? I'm at an abandoned house alone and you used a deep voice…" When she realized how uptight she was being, she got tickled and started laughing too. "You jerk!" she said when she caught her breath. "You're lucky I didn't have my pepper spray on me."

"Well, if you're going to come to abandoned houses, that's probably when you should bring your pepper spray."

"I wasn't planning to come here, actually. I was walking to work. And I'm late…" she said putting her hand over her mouth. "Gosh, where is my brain lately?"

"Relax. I just came from Jolt," he said, holding up a cup of coffee. "Rebecca's not very busy. Care to walk with me?"

She nodded and they made their way down the driveway and back out onto the street. With each passing day, January Cove was getting colder and colder. For full-time beach bums, the temperatures were hard on the regular citizens of the small town. They lived for spring and summer, as did most of the businesses. Some business owners took second jobs during the winter months just to make ends meet.

"So, no ferry riders this morning?" she asked as they passed the hardware store and then the ice cream shop.

"Not a one. I was hoping you might take a trip, but to no avail," he said with a smile.

"Nah, not today, my friend. I'm a working girl."

Clay started laughing. "You might not want to say that. It could be misinterpreted, ya know..."

"Haha. Very funny. You're a regular comedian."

She and Clay had always bantered back and forth. Even though he was older than her, she'd always been able to hold her own with him. The more he taunted and picked at her, the more sarcastic and fiery she became. She remembered him once asking if she died her hair because he was sure she was a red head underneath those curly brown locks of hers.

"Do you remember when our families went on that camping trip together?" Clay asked as they walked.

"Oh yes. I remember you pushing me in the lake very well!"

"I never pushed you in the lake!"

"Yes you did, you liar!" she said as she punched him in the arm. "We were in the canoe, and you told me to stand up. Of course, I didn't know any better and you pushed me in!"

"Um, that is not at all how I remember it, and I would never do anything that unchivalrous. I'm a Southern gentleman." He smiled that dimpled smile, and her stomach flipped. Or maybe the baby was moving.

"You might be a Southern gentleman now, but you pushed me in the dang lake back then."

"Okay, fine. I admit it. But I did it on a dare."

"A dare? With who?" she asked, knowing full well it was one of her brothers.

"I'm afraid for my physical safety if I say…."

"Sure you are! Come on. Who?"

"Brad."

"Brad? Oh, I'm going to smack him the next time I see him!"

"That'll make for a good Christmas picture," he said chuckling.

Clay was so easy to talk to. It was one of the things she'd admired about him ever since she was young. He would taunt her around her brothers, but he was always there to lend an ear when she wanted to talk about stuff. Usually boy stuff.

She remembered getting her heart broken by a boy in middle school, and Clay had been right there to pick up the pieces when he found her crying on the beach after school. She sure had done a lot of crying on the beach in her life, yet it was her favorite place on Earth.

They arrived at the front door of Jolt, and Addison said a quick goodbye to Clay before running inside and apologizing to Rebecca for being late. But she couldn't help herself and looked back to watch him walk up the street toward the ferry dock. And a small part of her wondered why she hadn't noticed Clay before now. Why did she ever leave January Cove and hook up with the likes of Jim?

~

IF THERE WAS one thing Aaron Parker knew, it was that he adored his girlfriend's son, Tyler. After just turning three years old, the kid had stolen his heart almost from the first moment they met. And today was no different.

As they sat together fishing off the dock of a local lake, Aaron couldn't imagine his life without this kid in it. Of course, having Tessa in his life wasn't a bad deal either. She was beautiful, smart and strong. She was honest to a fault and she seemed to always do the right thing no matter how hard it was. He admired her, and lately he didn't admire himself nearly as much.

"Hey, bro," he heard his brother, Brad yell from behind. "You not working today?" Brad was climbing out of his big, black pickup truck and Tyler ran to greet him with a bear hug.

"Uncle Brad!" he yelled. He called all the Parker brothers "uncle" now and thought of them as his own family. Tyler really didn't have any other family after his mother had left his abusive father.

"Hey, man. No, I just took the afternoon off. Tessa's running the counter at the campground so me and peanut here can go fishing," he said as he stood up and put his fishing pole in the little metal holder staked into the ground.

"Anything biting?"

"Not really. But that wasn't really the point," he said. Everyone knew Aaron loved spending time with Tyler, even if that meant sitting there without any fish biting. Having lost his Dad at a two years old, Aaron wanted to make sure that Tyler always had a father figure around who did those cool things with him. He planned to teach him how to shoot a bow and arrow, how to catch a football and eventually how to capture the attention a beautiful woman and make her his wife.

"Aaron, can I play on the swing?" he asked, pointing to the small swing set that was on the edge of the property.

"Yes, but stay where I can see you, okay?" Tyler nodded and ran off. "So what's up?" he asked Brad as he sat on the edge of a picnic table.

"Well, I wanted to talk about the bachelor party for Kyle."

"Jeez, man, that's months away. It's December. They aren't getting married until the spring. Aren't we jumping the gun a bit?" Aaron laughed.

"Hey, this is a big deal. The first Parker brother to get married!" Brad was the most animated of all the Parker kids, including Addison. He was a planner, but he was also outgoing and spontaneous when he needed to be. He was hysterically funny, and insanely curious to the point that most would've called him nosy. Everyone in the family thought he should've been a reporter instead of a contractor, but he stuck with the family business of real estate.

"Okay, so what were you thinking? Strippers and debauchery for twenty-four hours?" Aaron winked.

"I doubt that's a good plan since all of my brothers are tied down. Don't want to be responsible for Tessa kicking your butt to the curb," Brad said with a chuckle. Aaron smiled.

"Yeah, she'd probably put me in a headlock and throw me into that lake right there."

"So, how are things going with you guys anyway? Should I be expecting wedding bells from another brother anytime soon?" Brad asked in his usual nosy fashion.

"Do you always have to have your nose in my business?" Aaron asked, walking over and removing his fishing pole from the holder.

"Ooohh. Did I touch a nerve?"

"No, of course not. Things are great with me and Tessa." Aaron took the bait off his hook and tossed the rod into the back of his truck without looking at his brother.

"Dude, I'm your big brother. You know you can talk to me, right?" Brad said, suddenly serious.

Aaron took in a deep breath. "Seriously. Things are great. I'm just feeling the pressure with all this wedding talk. I know she wants to get engaged, and I think it's too soon. I mean, we've only been dating a few months." He leaned against the picnic table.

"Look, man, you don't need to feel pressured by any of this. You do what's right for you and Tessa, and that little guy over there."

"She's starting to talk about it, though, and I don't want to let her down. I just feel a little…. wary…"

"About Tessa? She's an awesome woman…"

"Not about her. About Natalie."

"Natalie? Where the hell did that come from?" Brad asked, talking a little too loudly. "You're not messing around on Tessa…" he whispered.

"Of course not!" Aaron snapped. "I meant about what Natalie did to me. I trusted her."

"And you're wondering how you'll know if you can trust Tessa?"

"Sort of. I don't know…"

"Aaron, there are no guarantees in life. Any woman can cheat on you. But she probably worries about you too."

"How?"

"Her husband beat on her, man. What's to say you don't turn out to be like him?"

"I would never do that!"

"You say that, but he probably said that too…"

"Are you saying I'll be a wife beater? Thanks, Brad."

"Of course I'm not saying that. Just making a point that she could be worried about you turning out like her ex while you're worrying about her turning out like your ex. You can't compare Tessa to Natalie. It's not fair, just like it wouldn't be fair for her to compare you to that louse of a husband she had."

He made a good point. Aaron smiled at the irony of it all.

"I've never thought of it like that."

"Well, I'm smart so I'm glad I could enlighten you."

"Shut up, you moron," Aaron said, punching his brother in the arm.

"Here's my last piece of wisdom… You have to decide whether Tessa and Tyler are worth the risk. Then you'll have your answer."

CHAPTER 8

s she did most mornings now, Addison found herself walking along the shoreline on her way to Jolt. She was starting to get a routine going now that she was back in January Cove, and that felt good since her life had been anything but routine in the last few months.

With Christmas just another week away, she felt secure where she was right now. Having her family around her was giving her much needed strength, but it didn't mean she doubted herself any less than she did before. The constant questions plagued her. The unknown parts of her life seemed to be the only certain thing she had.

She stared out into the ocean as the sun came up over the horizon. Another day. She was thankful for that. She quietly spoke to her baby, as she did a lot now, and promised to do her best to be a good mom.

"Good morning," she heard a male voice say from

behind her. Oh no. Who had heard her talking to her baby? More importantly, was it Clay? She turned.

"Good morning, Jackson," she said with a relieved smile. "You've got to stop scaring me like that."

"Here, I brought you a coffee and a muffin," he said as he plopped down on the sand. Since Addison could no longer "plop", she eased herself down onto the dry, cool sand and took the coffee and bagged muffin.

"Thanks. You already went to Jolt this morning?"

"Well, I do have an 'in' with the owner, you know," he said with a wink.

"Gross."

"I didn't mean it like that! Get your mind out of the gutter, sis," he said laughing. "I had an early morning conference call, so I needed some energy."

"I like Rebecca a lot. You really scored on that one, bro," she said. "She's been so supportive of me even when I get nauseous or mess up the cash register."

"She likes you too. And she understands, trust me."

"I'm glad she does because I don't. I wish I felt more like my old self, whatever that means." Addison took a sip of her coffee and looked down at her feet.

"Things will get better, Addy. They always do. This is just a season of your life, but it'll pass," he said putting his arm around her.

"It's just hard watching the total destruction of your marriage. It wasn't a good marriage, but it was mine and I thought my life would be different. Things haven't turned out at all like I'd planned."

"Life never turns out like we plan, but you gotta roll with it. I never expected to be back in January Cove.

Just like you, I thought I was destined for the big city life, but fate had other plans. I bet fate has other plans for you too."

"I hope so. I wish I could be more like Clay…"

Jackson choked on his coffee. "Clay?"

"Yeah. I've been spending more time with him lately, just running into him here and there. Didn't know he ran the ferry. Anyway… Clay has always known January Cove was his home, and he's never had ambitions to leave. I wish I hadn't left, but I know it was probably the best thing at the time."

"Well, don't have Clay's ambition-less mentality. I don't know how he makes ends meet with that ferry."

Addison smiled inside because she knew his secret, but she wasn't about to tell it to Jackson or anyone else. "It's hard to think about the future right now. All I can think about is the baby and getting this divorce behind me."

"But maybe you do need to think more about the future. What do you want to do with your life? I mean, what's your passion? Is it still decorating?" he asked as he bit into a large blueberry muffin.

"I do love decorating, but lately I've got another idea in my head that I can't seem to shake."

"What is it?"

"Well, if I had the money, I'd buy the old Mallory house and open a B&B." She waited for Jackson to sigh or roll his eyes, but it didn't happen. Her serious to a fault brother made no sound and then spoke.

"Then you should do it. Make a plan and go for your dream, Addy," he said softly.

"What? Who are you and what have you done with my very practical brother?"

"Look, I've learned a lot being with Rebecca even for this short period of time. She lost her husband in September 11th, and they thought they had all the time in the world before that. We don't know what the future holds, so I think we need to pursue our dreams when we can."

"But I can't, Jackson. I have no money and a baby on the way. My dreams need to go on the back burner."

"Maybe you can't buy the Mallory place, but what about just working for yourself? You've got months before the baby gets here. Why not take on some decorating jobs? Call your company back in Atlanta and see if they have some jobs you can take on. You can always drive up for the day and meet with clients."

Addison pondered the idea. It might work, so she would put it on her list of ideas.

"I might give that a try. Thanks, Jackson," she said leaning over and putting her head on his shoulder.

"Well, I hate to eat and run, but I've got that conference call in ten minutes."

She hugged him goodbye and started her own walk to Jolt. She had a few minutes, so she pulled our her cell phone to call the office and see if they had anything for her.

"Real Deal Decorating," her secretary, Amber, answered in her usual upbeat voice. Although she had worked on her own when she first arrived in Atlanta, Jim had invested into her opening Real Deal after she'd built her reputation.

"Hey, Amber. It's Addison," she said. There was a long pause before Amber spoke.

"Oh… hey…" She seemed to be stammering over her words.

"Listen, I was wondering if we have any open jobs I could work on…" she started to say, but Amber interrupted her.

"I'm sorry, Addison, but we don't."

"Nothing? But we had quite a few extra jobs before I left…"

"Look, Addison, you really need to talk to Jim about this."

"Jim? What's he got to do with this?"

"Well, from what we've been told, Jim was the investor backing this company and he just let you run things. Now that you're divorcing him, he's taken the reins." Her tone was snotty and sarcastic.

"Excuse me? Jim is running an interior design business? Seriously?"

"Actually, he hired a manager. She's running things, but he's in charge of the company."

"We ran that company together, Amber, and you know it. He can't just come in and take over!" Addison said through gritted teeth. She wasn't going to cry and give anyone that ammunition against her.

"You need to talk to Jim. Or maybe your attorney," Amber said, obviously brushing her off.

"Let me ask one more question before you hang up and gossip about me," Addison said.

"Fine. What?" Amber said, sounding about as interested as a preschooler would be in this conversation.

"Who's the manager?"

Amber paused before saying, "Tiffani." Then she hung up.

~

ADDISON MADE it to Jolt in the nick of time and ran behind the counter to put on her apron just as Rebecca finished ringing up a customer.

"You okay?" Rebecca asked as the customer left.

"Yeah. Just not a good morning," Addison said as she attempted to distract herself with wiping down the back counter.

"Can I help?"

"I doubt it. Unless you're a hired assassin and don't mind taking out my soon-to-be ex-husband?"

"No, sorry. My hired assassin days are far behind me. I own a coffee shop now," Rebecca said with a giggle. Addison followed with laughter and felt better. "So what's going on?"

Addison told her about the phone call to her interior design firm and how she was treated by her own former secretary. She also told her about the revelation that Tiffani was apparently back with Jim even though they'd supposedly broken up months ago. Of course, Jim wasn't exactly a truth-teller, so maybe they never broke up at all.

"Surely he can't just take the whole business?"

"You know, I don't even care. I don't ever want to go back there, and the business was floundering anyway. I'm sure he's doing everything he can to kill my professional name up there. I just want to start over. I don't ever want to see those people again," Addison said as she banged the tamper for the cappuccino machine against the side of the counter. Rebecca carefully took if from her and smiled.

"Why don't you sit down for a bit?" she said sweetly. Addison felt horrible. She wasn't a very good worker so far. She leaned against the counter and sighed.

"My life has really gone off the rails. I'd understand if you want to fire me, Rebecca. I really would."

"I'm not firing you! I love having you here, Addy. I'm glad it gives you something to do while you figure things out."

"I just feel so useless. I'm used to being in charge and always on the go."

"Maybe you need a hobby?" Rebecca suggested.

Addison laughed. "I've never been one for hobbies. Jackson suggested taking some freelance interior design work."

"That's a good idea too. I wish I hadn't already redecorated this place…"

"It's beautiful, Rebecca. You have a real eye for design."

"I doubt that," she said giggling. "Oh, look, here's one of my favorite customers now!"

The bell dinged on the door and an older man walked in. Addison knew everyone in town when she left years ago, but not this man. He was short and thin and had barely a few sprigs of white hair on top of his head. He ambled in using a cane.

"Hello, dear," the man said, giving Rebecca a kiss on the cheek as she leaned over the counter.

"Hello, Mr. Linden. What can I do for you today?"

"Oh, my usual, dear," he said. She nodded and started pouring a cup of coffee. "Mr. Linden, this is my friend and new co-worker, Addison Parker. Addison, this is my secret boyfriend, Mr. Paul Linden." Rebecca smiled and so did Mr. Linden.

"Well, we'd better not tell my wife about this," he said chuckling. "Hi there, Addison." Addison reached out and shook his hand.

"So what's your regular?" she asked, trying to get to know her new customer.

"Coffee black, bran muffin. Pretty easy really. Helps keep an old man regular," he said. More information than Addison needed.

"Hey, Mr. Linden, let me ask you something as a retired attorney…" Rebecca started.

"What's that?"

Rebecca regaled him with tales of Addison's marriage and upcoming divorce while she stood there with her mouth hanging open. Rebecca whispered to her, "Don't worry. He never remembers anything we talk about, but his advice is always on point."

When she was finished, he raised one of his bushy eyebrows and smiled.

"Well, I have to tell you that is an interesting story. And I find with stories like these that in order to get a happy ending, one must fight fire with fire. Your jackass of a husband needs a swift kick in the rear," he said. Addison nodded in agreement but let the old man talk. "You've got to get evidence, my dear. Evidence that he's been unfaithful, and that he did it first."

"But there is no evidence..." she started.

"Oh, dear, there's always evidence. One just has to know where to look."

"Unfortunately, he's got all the money. I can't afford a long, drawn out process..."

"Here," he said, reaching into his pocket and handing her a business card. "This is an old friend of mine. He's an ex-police officer turned private investigator who specializes in things like this. Tell him I sent you. He'll give you a deal, I promise."

"Thank you," she said, looking down at the card. The name was Harrison Gibbs.

"He can help you," the old man said as he took his coffee and bagged muffin. "See you tomorrow!"

Rebecca waved as Mr. Linden left. Addison had a twinkle of renewed hope. Maybe this Harrison Gibbs could help her make sure that Jim didn't win in the end.

~

ADDISON REACHED down into the big box, struggling to pull out the last of the ribbon. Her mother's over-decorating at the holidays was exhausting her today. After working at Jolt, she'd been immediately recruited to help get everything ready for the big Christmas festivities that were coming in just a few days.

"I can't believe I've got so many presents to wrap. All these new kids in the family this year have really put me behind," Adele said with a smile. "I can't wait to see Tyler open his building set. I hope Leo likes those jeans. Rebecca said they were his favorite kind. And giving Kaitlyn the circus tickets is going to be a big shocker for her!" Adele was simply giddy with Christmas cheer.

"You really love the holidays, don't you, Mom?" Addison said, laughing as her mother went crazy curling the ribbons.

"Oh, sweetie, I adore this time of year! And this year all of my kids are together which makes it even more special. Of course, next year we'll have your little bundle and maybe we can get Brad a date."

"Hey!" Brad called from the kitchen where he was hanging garland across the breakfast area. "I heard that!"

"I was hoping you did," she said sweetly as she continued wrapping. Brad had been the only one she could rope into helping on this day.

"Listen, Mom, I hope you don't mind but I invited someone over for tea today. He's a private investigator that a customer at Jolt recommended. He might be able to help me with my divorce case."

"A private investigator? What's he going to do?" she asked as she stopped wrapping and looked at her daughter.

"Well, I need to prove that Jim cheated first basically. Otherwise, I'm sunk. He'll get everything because he knows I don't want him spreading rumors all over town about me. Although I don't know why I even care. I guess it's the principle of the thing."

"Then we'll do what we need to do. If a P.I. is what you need, then I support that. Let's sock it to him!" she said, holding her scissors in the air as if to signal the beginning of a battle.

Addison laughed. Her mother had always been her biggest cheerleader.

The doorbell rang about a half an hour later just as Addison finished helping her mother. She asked Adele to start some tea and opened the door to find a very handsome older man standing there. She wasn't sure what she'd expected. Maybe some guy in a trench coat. But this guy was "dapper" with a nice suit and thick brown hair with specks of gray in it. He was broad shouldered and looked more like an elegant news anchor or Hollywood celebrity than he did an ex-cop.

"Addison?" he said, his voice as smooth as his appearance.

"That's me. Nice to meet you," she said, reaching out and shaking his hand. "Come on in."

He entered the home and followed Addison into the breakfast area.

"Mom, I want you to meet..." Addison started.

"Harrison? Is that you? Harrison Gibbs?" Adele said, staring at him like she'd seen a ghost.

"Adele Parker? I thought you used to live around here, but I had no idea this was your house! I should've put two and two together, I guess," he said laughing. Adele came from around the breakfast bar and embraced him tightly.

"It's so good to see you!" she said looking up at him. "And how's Elaine?"

"Oh, Elaine and I divorced years ago. It's one of the reasons I like to help ladies in Addison's situation. I hate cheaters," he said, raising his eyebrow.

"I'm so sorry, Harrison," Adele said frowning. "I always thought Elaine was a lovely woman."

"I did too, and so did several other gentlemen," he said with a chuckle. "It's been many years ago, and I understand she's on her fourth marriage now."

"Wow," Adele said, making a tsk tsk sound with her tongue. "I just can't believe what a small world it is!"

"Um, excuse me, folks, but can someone explain… this?" Addison asked. Harrison and Adele laughed.

"Sorry, sweetie. Harrison and your father were dear friends a long time ago, but we haven't seen each other in many, many years. When was the last time we saw each other?"

"I think it was about a year after he died. Elaine and I ran into you at Seewald's before we moved," he said, referring to the old grocery store that used to be in January Cove.

"That's right. Wow, that's a long time."

"It is. You look wonderful, Adele. The years have certainly been kind to you," he said, and Addison couldn't help but feeling like the third wheel even though she'd invited him over. An uncomfortable silence hung in the air.

"Well, I don't want to hold you up any longer than necessary, Mr. Gibbs," Addison said, pointing to a chair at the table.

"Please, call me Harrison," he said with a warm

smile as he took a seat. "Are you going to join us, Adele?"

She smiled. It was a smile Addison had never seen on her mother before. Was that a flirtatious smile she just saw?

"Sure. If Addison doesn't mind…"

"I don't mind," Addison said, feeling more like she was chaperoning two high school kids than sitting with a private investigator.

"Now, Addison, you told me a little about your husband, but what I need to know is all the places you know he traveled during the time period he was with Tiffani. The earlier the better."

"Well, I don't know if he was where he said he was…"

"Come up with a list of places that you know he likes to frequent. Restaurants, coffee houses, offices, parks, vacation spots, and so forth. I have lots of contacts in Atlanta who can help me comb over surveillance video to see if we can catch anything untoward that will help your case. Given what you've told me thus far, I bet we can catch him in enough of a compromising situation to get the leverage you need." He took a sip of his tea and winked at Adele. What was that?

"Really? So there's hope?" Addison asked.

"There's always hope," he said with a smile. "Trust me. Guys like him think they're above the law, so he probably got sloppy somewhere along the way. He thought he had you snowed, so I doubt he was very careful."

"He did have me snowed."

"No. You were a caring, devoted wife who trusted her husband. You did nothing wrong."

"Actually, I did do something wrong."

"Well, maybe not the best decision ever made, but you reacted to something very upsetting, Addison," Adele interjected.

They sat and talked for another twenty minutes or so, and Addison really liked Harrison Gibbs. He seemed kind and cordial and laid back. And Adele seemed interested. Very interested.

"Listen, I've got to run an errand, but it was so nice meeting you, Harrison. I can't wait to see what you find. Mom, you'll see him out?" she asked, smiling slyly behind Harrison's head.

"Of course, dear," Adele said pursing her lips and trying not to smile back.

∽

ADDISON WALKED with purpose as she headed toward the ferry. Maybe she would get some money out of her divorce settlement after all. At least she had some renewed hope because Harrison Gibbs seemed to think there may be evidence somewhere. And she hoped with everything she had that he'd find it.

Thoughts of the Mallory house danced through her head, and she made sure to spot the for sale sign still sitting in the yard as she passed it on the way to the ferry. She had to tell Clay the good news. He was becoming her best friend in town, and he understood her dream of owning a B&B.

"Hey!" she called as she walked down the dock. He was typing up the ferry and smiled as he waved at her. He looked especially hot today with his gray Henley shirt and form hugging jeans.

"Hey yourself! What are you doing down here so late in the day?"

"I have some good news. Well, actually I just have news, but I wanted to share it with someone."

"And you picked me? I feel so honored," he said grinning with his hand over his heart. "What's up?"

"Well, I met with a private investigator today and he thinks he might be able to get enough dirt on Jim to get him to back down a little. If that happens, I might get enough money to open my B&B!" she said smiling, being careful to keep her sweater tightly pulled over her belly.

"That's great, Addison!" he said walking over and hugging her tightly. Could he feel her expanding stomach? She sure hoped not, so she pulled away quickly and readjusted her sweater.

"You closing up for the day?"

"Yep. Didn't have any passengers after lunch, so I figured I was wasting my time. But I'm so glad you came before I left."

"Well, thanks for listening. Have a good night," she said as she started to turn.

"Hey..."

"Yeah?"

"You want to have dinner with me?"

CHAPTER 9

*A*ddison had never been to Clay's house before, only his parents' house. He lived just a few doors down from them even now, probably to help his mother with his father's health issues.

He lived in a small cottage style house right off the main road. It looked like a dollhouse and not nearly as manly as Addison would've expected. Of course, what does a "manly" house look like anyway?

Sometimes she was thankful that January Cove was small enough to walk most places, but today she hadn't worn the proper shoes for such a long walk. Pregnancy was doing a number on her feet as it was. She was petite in build anyway, so the little bit of added weight was wreaking havoc on her arches. Of course, she wasn't quite ready to let the cat out of the bag to Clay just yet.

It wasn't that she was intentionally trying to hide it. She just liked having someone to talk to who would listen and not look at her as some kind of charity case single mother-to-be.

"Come on in," he said as he unlocked the door and flipped on a lamp on a table by the front door.

"Wow. This is a beautiful place. Did you remodel it yourself?" she asked, looking around at the intricate woodwork and shiny hardwood floors.

"I did about three years ago. I love working with my hands," he said. "Please, sit down." He pointed to an overstuffed arm chair that sat by the mostly useless fireplace. January Cove got chilly, but usually not cold enough to warrant a fire.

Clay disappeared into the kitchen for a few moments, but came back with two glasses of iced sweet tea, a Southern staple. Any good Southern girl had better know how to make proper sweet tea. Addison had once traveled up north with Jim and asked for sweet tea in a restaurant. The server looked at her like she had two heads, and it was the first time she realized that the South was the only place she'd get her favorite beverage.

"Oh, thank you," she said, taking a sip. "Hey, you make fantastic sweet tea for a guy!"

"My momma taught me right, Addy," he said with a wink as he sat down on the sofa across from her.

"This place really is amazing. I love this table," she said, running her hand over the carved wood coffee table. "Where'd you get this?"

"I made it," he said, taking a sip of his tea.

She almost choked on her tea. "No you didn't!"

"Yes, I did," he said smiling. "I have a shop out back where I tinker around."

"You are so talented, Clay. You should be selling this stuff down on Main Street. Maybe you could get some space in the hardware store..."

"Oh, it's just a sideline, really. I don't have much time between my websites and the ferry business. It just gives me something to do as a hobby."

"Well, if I ever get to open my B&B, I want a custom piece made by you! You just name the price."

"The price for you will always be free, Addy," he said with a soft smile. There seemed to be some hidden meaning in it, but he quickly changed the subject before Addison could think too much about it. "So, tell me, do you still have an obsession with all things Gone With The Wind?"

Addison smiled. How had he remembered that about her? She was the only girl who, in eighth grade, redecorated her bedroom in every GWTW memento she could find. She even had a six foot Rhett Butler poster on her wall that would scare all of her friends when they woke up at her house after a sleepover.

"Of course! Rhett was my first love, after all. How did you remember that anyway?"

Clay shrugged his shoulders, brushing it off. "Good memory, I guess. Hey, what kind of music do you like?"

"I like anything really. Some new country, pop... Why?" she asked. His questions were pretty random.

"I like to cook and dance, so I wasn't sure what music to put on," he said as he stood and turned on the TV, searching for the Pandora app.

"You like to cook and dance?" she laughed. "That's... interesting...."

"It makes the tedious work of cooking more fun. You should try it!"

"I think I'll watch you, and that might be more entertaining," she said.

"Oh no... Not at my house," he said. "You must participate in the rhythm of the music," he said, laughing as he grabbed her hand and pulled her into the kitchen with country music blaring on the TV. "Do you know how to two step?"

"Um, no...." she said, unsure of what had overtaken her normally subdued friend.

"It's like this," he said as he put one hand on her waist and held her other hand. Before she knew it, they were moving around the kitchen floor and she was having fun. Surely, the baby was wondering what the heck was going on, but at least this dance didn't require close proximity where he could feel her secret baby bump.

As they danced, she was struck by his smile. Clay's teeth were perfect, but it was the emotion behind the smile that got to her. He was so genuine and good that it almost took her breath away. And his eyes twinkled, which reminded her of Santa Claus and almost made her laugh. She felt his hand on her waist and worried that he might feel her baby bump, but he kept it firmly in place. And then she felt her hand holding his hand and something about that felt very right and very scary at the same time.

When the song ended, Addison sank down onto a

bar stool and smiled. "Why don't I remember us having fun like this when we were young?"

"Because you were always too young," he said with a sly smile. "There might be just a few years difference in our ages, but your brothers would've taken me out behind the wood shed if I'd even looked cross eyed at you, Addison."

"True, and they aren't much better now. I'm holding them off from killing Jim at the moment."

"Well, I'd have to agree with them on that one. In fact, if they form a posse, I'll join up."

She laughed. "No posse forming, please. I've got enough stress as it is."

"You like hamburgers?" he asked as he stuck his head in the refrigerator.

"Of course."

"Then, let me go start the grill."

She observed him as he flipped the burgers, cut up potatoes and moved around the kitchen like a pro. She and Jim had never cooked together. Not even once. Jim considered cooking to be "woman's work", so Addison spent her time alone in the kitchen trying to please his palate.

A little while later, they were finished up with an amazing dinner of hamburgers and fresh cut fries followed by a chocolate pie he had in the freezer. She could tell he didn't entertain much since he had little food in the refrigerator, and there weren't any feminine touches around the house.

When they retired to the living room, Addison

decided to find out more about Clay and what his life had been like since she'd last seen him.

"I don't understand something," she started.

"What?"

"Well, you're a good looking, smart guy who can make furniture like this, drive a ferry and run businesses. You own your own home, you love your mother and you're a pretty good dancer."

"Where are you going with this?" he asked chuckling.

"Why hasn't some woman snagged you yet?"

The look on his face was a mixture of shock and uncertainty, as if he was biting his tongue. She couldn't place just what it was, but she knew it was there and it confused the heck out of her.

"Just haven't found the right one yet, I guess," he said softly.

"No, that's too simple an answer, Clay Hampton. Do you even date?"

"Occasionally. Not a lot of choices in January Cove, Addy."

"What about that Samantha chick?" she asked, a strange feeling of jealousy brewing in her stomach. Or was that the hamburger? Either way, it was an uncomfortable feeling.

"It was okay while it lasted, but Samantha just wasn't my type in the end. She wanted a different kind of life. A 'big life' as she called it. Not interested in building a family with me here, and I wasn't interested in jet setting across the world with her."

"I hope you find the right woman for you soon, Clay."

"I do too," he said, a hint of a smile playing on his lips. Just enough to show one dimple. Why did she want to stick her tongue in that dimple so badly?

"Well, thanks for dinner. I really better get home. I have to go shopping with the girls tomorrow."

"Shopping, huh? Sounds terribly boring." She laughed.

"We girls like that kind of thing."

"Come on, I'll drive you home," he said as he stood and pulled the keys out of his pocket.

"No, you really don't have to. It's not a long walk." Her feet were screaming at her already.

"Addison, do you not know me any better than that?"

"What?"

"I'm a Southern gentleman, and even Rhett Butler wouldn't let a lady walk home at dark. Now, your carriage awaits!" he said in his best thick Southern accent as he jutted out his elbow toward her. She linked her arm through his, a rush of electricity shooting through her.

They drove up in front of the Parker house and Addison turned to him. "Thanks so much for dinner and for driving me home. It's been so nice getting to know you as an adult, Clay."

His expression was soft, and she found herself staring at his incredible lips. She really needed to ask her doctor about those pesky pregnancy hormones as soon as possible, she decided.

"It was my pleasure. Have a good night's sleep and enjoy your shopping tomorrow," he said. Shopping. The trip was to buy pregnancy clothes. Jenna and Tessa were taking her.

Addison climbed out of the truck and smiled and waved before disappearing into the protective confines of her home. She needed to put some distance between her and Clay before she lost control of herself. The last thing she needed was to fall for her childhood friend right now. She wasn't even divorced yet, was carrying another man's baby and fantasizing about her friend.

Note to self: Google about pregnancy hormones. Stat!

∾

CLAY HAMPTON WAS TIED up in knots. On the one hand, he'd promised his friends that he wasn't going to pursue their sister. On the other hand, he'd been vexed by her since they were young. There was always a brick wall in their path. She was too much younger than him. She was dating someone else. She got married. Clay had never had a chance, and he couldn't help but wonder whether his chance was right now.

He sat at the Jake's Bar staring into the glass of beer, already missing his time with Addison. It was crazy. He hadn't seen her in years, but he'd never forgotten her and asked about her every chance he got. He tried to do it nonchalantly, but he was pretty sure at least Jackson knew something was amiss.

"Drinking alone?" he heard Jackson say from behind him. His ears must have been burning.

"Just chilling out," Clay said without turning around.

Turns out, Jackson wasn't alone. Brad slapped him on the back.

"We need to talk," Jackson said as the two men sat on both sides of him. This wasn't going anywhere good.

"What's up?" Clay asked, taking a swig of his beer.

"At the risk of sounding like a gangster, I thought I warned you," Jackson said as he pointed at the bartender and ordered two more beers.

"Warned me about what?" Clay said trying not to make eye contact.

"You know what, Clay. Don't try to BS me, man. We know you spent the evening with our sister."

"Don't make it sound raunchy, dude. We had dinner at my house. And then we had a sex party."

"Very funny," Jackson said as the bartender slid a beer in front of him and then Brad.

"Look, she came down to the ferry to talk to me about something. I was closing up and didn't want to make her walk all the way back home, so I invited her to dinner."

"Clay, you can't string her along or take this in the direction you want. Things are too…. complicated… for her right now," Brad said.

Clay felt like they weren't telling him something, but he was too angry to delve into it. Who were they to tell him who he could and couldn't see anyway?

"Look, man, I see the way you look at my little sister. You always have," Jackson started. "She's not available right now. Just trust me on that."

"She's still married. I know that. We're just friends, guys. Trust me on that," Clay said sarcastically.

"You know what your problem is?" Brad said taking a sip of his beer. "You need a woman."

Clay chuckled. "You're one to talk. When's the last time you had a date?"

Brad shrugged. "We're not here to talk about me."

"Well, I'm not here to talk about me either," Clay said as he stood up and slapped a few bucks on the counter.

"Don't be mad, man," Brad said. Jackson said nothing and glared at his friend instead. What the hell was wrong with these guys? They were like his brothers, but suddenly he was the outcast.

Jackson finally spoke. "Clay, you're like a brother to us, and we don't want to see you get hurt or caught up in something that isn't your fight."

"If this is about Jim, I can handle that jackass," he said. Neither of them spoke. "I gotta go check on my Mom before bed. See ya'll later." He walked out, completely determined to ask Addison for a date sooner rather than later. No one was going to tell him who he could see, including his best friends.

∼

ADDISON STOOD in front of the mirror and turned to the side. Her belly seemed to have expanded in the last few hours. She wasn't going to be able to hide this pregnancy much longer, and she really didn't want to.

She'd had a lot of time to think after Clay dropped her off, and it left her wondering why she was hiding her pregnancy in the first place. She wasn't ashamed of her baby, and she wasn't really ashamed of herself as much anymore. Her actions hadn't been right, for sure, but she had to accept what she'd done and move on. It was the only way to find peace.

Her cell phone rang and startled her, and she could've sworn the baby jumped too. It was crazy to feel movement in there now.

"Hello?" she said.

"Hey." The voice was unmistakable. Clay.

"Oh, hey! Everything okay?" He sounded tired.

"Of course. Listen, I just wanted to tell you how much fun I had tonight. You were a great dinner companion."

She smiled. "You don't get out much, do you?" she said as she sat down on the edge of her bed.

"You're a lot of fun, Addy. Always have been."

"Thanks," she said, feeling a little unsettled and curious about the reason for his call.

"I'm calling because I wanted to ask you a question."

"Okay…"

"Would you consider having dinner with me again sometime?" He sounded almost nervous.

"I'd love to. We'll have to plan that soon," she said softly.

"Great. I'll be in touch."

Addison hung up the phone and realized the butterflies she was currently feeling in her stomach had nothing at all to do with her baby.

~

THE NEXT MORNING, Addison went shopping with Tessa and Jenna. Addy wanted "non-maternity-looking maternity clothes" which were basically just big sweaters and leggings. And her belly still showed.

This wasn't as much about hiding the pregnancy as it was about not wanting to get too fat. Addison had always been petite, and it was the one thing she loved about herself right now. She'd never struggled with weight, much to her friends' dismay. But now she couldn't control her figure at all.

As she was checking out at one of the stores, the cashier told her about a prenatal yoga class that was going on at a local church. She broke off from Jenna and Tessa to try out a class, hoping that she wouldn't see anyone she knew. The church was one county over, which was a bit of a drive, but allowed her some anonymity for awhile. She could just be a new mommy-to-be instead of a pregnant woman in hiding.

Truthfully, she would be glad when the secret was out. Hiding it was becoming exhausting, and she wasn't even sure why she was still hiding it! Procrastination had always been her one pitfall. It was probably how she ended up married to Jim for so long in the first place - she just kept putting off the inevitable.

It was nice to hang out with other pregnant women, just talking about their babies. She was about to become a member of a new club - the "mommy club". The thought made her heart smile. One day soon, someone would say "mommy" and they'd be referring to her.

As Addison was walking to her car, her phone rang. She threw her purse onto the hood of her small car and started digging. Organization was never one of her strong suits.

"H... Hello?" she said, trying not to drop it as she struggled to press the button.

"Hey, Addy," she heard Clay say. Something about his voice made her stomach immediately do a somersault.

"Hey," she said as she unlocked her car and sat down. "How are you?"

"I'm good. And you?"

This conversation felt very tentative, like they were both walking on eggshells. Really, there was no reason for it. No matter how he made her feel, he was her friend, plain and simple. Her life was far too complicated to include a man - any man - in it right now. And Clay was too wonderful to wait around for her. Some woman needed to snap him up.

"I'm good."

"How was your shopping trip?" he asked with a laugh. She could hear seagulls in the background. He must be at the ferry, she thought.

"Very fun. It always is with those ladies, though," she giggled.

"I'd love to be a fly on the wall."

"No, you wouldn't. It'd probably bore you to death."

"I always have fun when I'm with you, Addison. Boring isn't possible."

Her heart jumped into her throat. Was he flirting with her?

He cleared his throat, anxiety apparent in his voice. "Listen, I was just wondering if you might like to have dinner again tomorrow night?"

"I'd love to," she heard herself saying. What was she doing?

"Great. I was thinking we could grill some steaks. Maybe watch a movie? Or, if you want, we can go eat at a restaurant..."

"No, no... I enjoyed being at your place, actually," she said, knowing that the less people she saw the better.

"Oh. Great," he stammered. "How about seven?"

"I'll be there!" she said, struggling not to say "It's a date!"

When she hung up the phone, she couldn't help but feel that she'd done just that - made a date with Clay Hampton. They were slowly creeping out of the "friend zone" and straight into something else. But he didn't know her secret, and stringing him along wasn't something she was prepared to do. No, she'd have to tell Clay something soon, and certainly before anything could happen between them.

CHAPTER 10

Sometimes, things happen that you don't expect. And sometimes, those things aren't good.

Addison had no idea that filling in for Rebecca on her day off would turn into a not so good day.

It started like any other normal day at Jolt, with the regulars coming in for coffee and breakfast before their work days. Even Clay breezed through for his coffee, but he was in a hurry since he actually had ferry riders that morning.

After the breakfast rush, Addison did what she normally did which was clean up around the counter. Christmas was just three days away, and Jolt would be closed both Christmas Eve and Christmas Day, so this would be the last big cleaning before that.

She had her back turned to the front door while she worked out her frustrations with life on the cappuccino machine. The bell dinged, and she didn't even turn around.

"Welcome to Jolt!" she said in her friendliest voice before she turned.

Standing there was the devil himself. Jim.

"Well, hello, barista Addison," he said with a sarcastic smile on his face. "Moving up in the world, I see."

"Get out, Jim," she seethed. Instead, he slapped a stack of papers down on the counter.

"You sign here, and I'll leave and never come back."

She stared at the papers, determined not to cry. "I'm not signing anything. I've already told you that."

"Are you stupid? You're going to lose your credibility when everybody finds out what a whore you are."

"Whore? What about you, Jim? You were screwing Tiffani for months! What does that make you?" she yelled, pointing in his face.

"A stud, I suppose," he said chuckling in that maniacal manner that made her wonder if he was mentally stable.

"No, it makes you a philandering bastard, that's what it makes you. I can't believe I ever wasted a moment on a sorry jackass like you," she said, her eyes squinted as she stared him down. "And the crazy thing is I would've stayed with you forever because I took my vows seriously. I would've continued sleeping with you even though it was never good and you were seriously 'shortchanged' in some departments, if you know what I mean..."

He reached across the counter and grabbed her forearm, pinning it to the countertop. "Listen up, you bitch, I'm not messing around here. You understand?

Sign the damn papers!" Shock overwhelmed her. Jim had never been physically abusive, but he looked like he could kill her right now.

She jerked as hard as she could but couldn't extract her arm. "Let me go or you'll be sorry."

"Ooh... I'm scared..." he said laughing. What he didn't see was her brother Kyle outside of the glass window. But he did feel him when Kyle yanked him by the hair a few moments later and threw him into the opposite wall.

"What the hell do you think you're doing to my sister?" Kyle asked through gritted teeth as he pressed Jim to the wall holding the back of his shirt collar in a knot.

"Just working out some business," Jim said with a smile, his face pressed against the wall.

"Kyle, just let him leave. Don't get yourself in trouble..." Addison pleaded. "Jim, you get out of here right now. If you don't, I'll have you locked up."

"Whatever," he said as Kyle released his grip. "This isn't over." He walked over to the counter and took the papers, smoothing out his shirt in the process. He looked down at Addison's expanding stomach which had slipped out around her apron. "Well, well, well.... I see the baby is growing well. What does it feel like to have physical evidence of your whore behavior?"

"Get out!" Kyle yelled as he rushed Jim again. Jim held his hands up and grinned.

"Chill, man. I'm going..." he walked to the door and turned around, ready to unleash one more piece of his wisdom. "You know, it's sad, really. You were such a beautiful woman at one time. You could've had any man you wanted. But now no one will want a dried up old slut like you. Once they realize what you really are, no one will want you." With that parting shot, Jim walked out and drove his BMW down the street.

And Addison was left wondering if he was right about that.

~

IT WAS 7:15. Her phone kept ringing and there were a couple of texts. She knew they were from Clay, but she couldn't bear to answer them. He was probably worried, and then he was probably angry when he realized she'd stood him up.

It was the only way. She couldn't explain right now. She was too upset.

Jim was right. She was used goods that no one else would want, and even if Clay thought he wanted her right now, he'd realize soon enough that she wasn't worth the effort.

Thankful that her brother promised not to tell her mother that Jim had shown up at Jolt, at least Addison could be sure she wouldn't add more stress to Adele. At least her Christmas could be joy filled.

She slipped out of the house and down onto the beach, wrapped in her favorite fleece blanket. Time alone was what she needed right now, and she'd apologize to Clay later.

She walked down to the shoreline, just outside of where the water could touch her toes and sat down.

Today, even the ocean wasn't soothing her soul. She felt so out of sorts, so lost. Why was this all so hard?

"Did you honestly think I wouldn't find you here?" she heard a voice behind her say. For a second, she worried it was Jim again. But it was Clay, and in some ways that was a harder pill to swallow. She wasn't ready to see him yet.

"Clay, I just can't do this right now…" she said without standing up. He quietly sat down beside her and looked out at the water.

"If you didn't want to eat my cooking again, you could've just said so," he said. A sarcastic smile played across his lips as he looked at her.

"I wanted to come. And I'm sorry I stood you up. I just had a rough day." She sighed.

"I know about Jim's little visit, Addy."

"How do you know?" she asked, turning to look at him.

"Kyle told me when I ran into him outside of Jolt. I tried to come find you then, but you were already gone. Don't shut me out, Addy," he said softly.

"Clay, this isn't your problem. It's bad enough I'm dragging my own family down. I'm not pulling you down with me too." She stood and started walking slowly down the waterline being careful to keep her blanket tight around her.

Clay followed her. "Jim's lucky that Kyle was there."

"Oh yeah? How so?" she asked, smiling up at him as they walked.

"Because if I'd been there, he would be wearing two

concrete blocks as shoes and taking a long nap in the ocean." Addison laughed.

"You'd turn mobster for me, Clay?"

"I'd do a lot of things for you, Addison Parker." She felt her heart flutter, but decided not to probe that question further. It would only lead him on and hurt him in the end.

"You know, seeing Jim brought back so many memories. At first, I really thought he was the one. He's a great salesman. He sold me on being with him. But marriage with Jim wasn't easy. It was hard. And lonely. As I sat out here on this beach alone, I realized that I'm not lonely here in January Cove. I feel surrounded by love and support even when I'm sitting here alone. And with Jim, I was surrounded by people and felt lonely. Go figure."

"You are surrounded by support and love here, Addison. Your home is here and has always been here," he said, touching her arm and turning her to face him. He was gentle, tentative, but she stopped and turned.

"I'm realizing that. Home will always be January Cove."

Clay smiled. "I'm glad I won't lose you again to the big city."

"Lose me?"

"Damn, Addy, do I have to hire a skywriter for you to see it?" he asked, running his hand through his thick, dark hair in frustration. Before she could answer, he continued. "I've wanted to pursue you since you were about eighteen years old. Your brothers have always warned me off, and I respected that. But you're the one I want. You're a part of my heart and always have been."

She couldn't breathe. She literally couldn't suck in a breath. "Wh...What?" she managed to finally choke out.

"I've been waiting for you, Addy," he said softly as he finally reached out and brushed her cheek with his thumb. "I kept waiting for you to realize who Jim really was, and I can't say I'm sorry your marriage fell apart. He doesn't deserve you, and I'm not sure I do either."

His words hit her like a lightning bolt. He'd been waiting for her? What did that even mean?

"Clay, this isn't right..." she stammered, taking his hand and putting it back down at his side. "You don't know who I really am. Yes, Jim's a terrible guy, but I'm not a good person myself."

"Addison, that's not true. You're the best person I know."

"You don't know the real me," she said softly, looking down at the sand. He put his index finger under her chin and lifted her eyes to his.

"I know you say you love Gone With The Wind, but really you love Rhett Butler. I know your favorite color is sky blue. I know you love blueberry pancakes with bacon crushed up in the batter. I know you love the smell of pine needles. I know you broke your arm at thirteen jumping on Jennifer Smart's trampoline. I know you learned to drive a stick shift, but ripped the clutch out of your brother's truck and had to finish learning on an automatic. I know you want to visit Italy one day...."

"How do you remember all that?" she asked, looking at him puzzled.

"Because I've made it my business to know you, Addison. Even when you weren't physically here, I kept you here," he said, putting his hand over his heart. "I realize this is a lot to take in, and you're just catching up. But I felt like this was my chance to let you know that there's one man on this Earth who sees you for who you are and loves everything about you. All the quirks, all the sarcasm, all the running away. I'm here, Addy. And your brothers might give me my own pair of concrete shoes before it's over with, but you needed to know and I needed to say it."

Before she could speak, he pulled her in closer and pressed his warm lips against hers, the waves crashing in the background as their lips crashed together. She kissed him back, enjoying his taste and softness, as she weaved her fingers through his hair. He wasn't taking anything from her, she was willingly giving it. His hands slid under her blanket, making their way around her side and to her lower back. And then he froze.

As if in slow motion, her blanket fell away and she stood there. Clay looked down and saw her pregnant stomach and time stood still.

~

THEY STOOD there in silence for a moment, Clay staring down at her belly and Addison staring at Clay.

"Say something," Addison whispered.

"What do you want me to say? How about why

were you hiding this from me?" he asked, stepping back and putting his hands on his hips. "You didn't trust me?"

"It had nothing to do with that, Clay. I'm embarrassed." She picked up the blanket and wrapped it back around her.

"Embarrassed? Because Jim got you pregnant and then abandoned you?"

She took in a deep breath and sighed. "No. Embarrassed because this isn't Jim's baby, Clay."

The look of shock on his face was painful to Addison. She'd just shattered all of the good things he thought of her. Shattered all of those sweet memories he had. Shattered her "good girl" image in his eyes. Another man who was disappointed in who she really was. A whore, according to Jim at least.

"What?" he said softly.

"When Jim cheated, I left him and got a job bartending. Some guy paid me attention, and I was craving it so badly at that time. I made a mistake, but the guy wants nothing to do with this. And that's why I'm getting smeared in my divorce. Jim has no problem proving my infidelity, and he's using this as leverage to ruin my professional reputation too. That's why I came home, and that's why my brothers are trying to protect me... and you."

It felt so good to get all of it off her chest, but at the same time she felt like she was hammering the nails into her own coffin. She'd never get a chance at happiness with Clay. And it was for the best. He needed a woman without so much baggage.

"I don't know what to say, Addison," he said. She hated not hearing "Addy" come out of his mouth. And how was it possible that she already missed his kisses?

"You don't have to say anything, Clay. Just walk away while you can."

And he did. Moments later, she was watching Clay Hampton walk straight out of her life.

~

CLAY HAD NEVER PUNCHED a hole in his wall before, but he stood there looking at two of them. One in the kitchen and one in the hallway. He wasn't normally an angry guy, but right now he was full of rage. At Jim for treating Addy the way he did. At the mystery guy who got her pregnant and ran out on her and his baby. And mostly at himself for leaving her standing there on the beach.

He hadn't wanted to walk away, but she seemed to need space. Now he regretted it. Maybe he just didn't know what to say and took the coward's way out.

And then there was that last little part of him that was saying maybe she was right. Maybe he did need to walk away while he could.

Moments later, a third hole shattered the quiet of his home.

Note to self: Buy a punching bag.

~

ADDISON WOKE up the next morning to the sound of Christmas music playing throughout the house. It was December 23, the day that her mother officially started her Christmas celebration.

Today, they would spend the day decorating cookies with the little kids and finish wrapping presents. Everyone would come over and spent the next couple of nights as a family, drinking hot apple cider in the evenings and probably playing a few board games.

This year would include Jenna and Kaitlyn, Tessa and Tyler and Rebecca and Leo which meant a lot more hustle and bustle in the Parker household. Addison was thankful for the needed distraction of family because all she'd been able to think about all night was Clay and the look on his face when she'd told him what a horrible person she was.

She took a quick shower and dressed in her favorite red Christmas sweater and new maternity jeans. Today was the day she would stop hiding.

It was almost as if the baby knew that she was out of hiding mode because she got the swiftest kick in the belly as she brushed through her hair.

"Hey!" she said, rubbing her belly and smiling. "Merry Christmas to you too."

She walked downstairs to find her mother in the kitchen, cooking ingredients spread everywhere.

"Good morning, dear," her mother said smiling as "Rockin' Around The Christmas Tree" played on Pandora.

"Good morning. Getting an early start I see?" Addison said giggling.

"Of course! Kaitlyn and Tyler will be here soon. Leo will follow later because he's too cool to make cookies, you know."

Leo was Rebecca's almost fifteen year old son and was way too hip to be making cookies with adults all day. She'd talked to him a few times in passing at Jolt and he seemed to be a good kid, but a teenager nonetheless. Jackson spent a lot of time with him, though, and Addison knew Rebecca was thankful for that.

"Can I help?" Addison asked.

"Sure. Maybe you can start mixing the batter?" Adele said, handing Addison the mixer and a bowl of ingredients. "I need to get to work on the other desserts for tomorrow and Christmas Day."

"Mom, do we really need so many sweets?"

"Honey, you're pregnant. Now's the time to eat sweets and enjoy!"

"I don't want to weigh four hundred pounds and have gestational diabetes!" Addison laughed.

They spent hours in the kitchen, later joined by most of the family, making cookies and cakes until it was lunchtime.

~

CLAY DIDN'T KNOW what to do with himself. He wouldn't have ferry passengers for several days as Christmas was so close. Normally, he spent half of Christmas Day with his parents and the other half with the Parkers. He'd done this for as long as he could remember.

But this year he wasn't sure he could.

Looking at Addison, especially after that kiss, was an impossible thought. That kiss had been everything he'd ever hoped and more, cementing the idea in his head that she was definitely "the one", as his mother called it.

No other woman would ever be able to compare to her. The way she made him feel. The way she looked. The way her hair smelled. Everything about her was what he wanted. Even the baby inside of her was what he wanted.

But he'd ruined it by leaving her standing there on the beach. When she'd needed him to understand and still be there, he'd left. Like all the other men in her life, he'd disappeared. First, her father died and left Addison without a Daddy growing up. Then her husband had betrayed her. When Clay had finally had his chance, he had let her down.

He had to do something besides punching holes in his walls, so he grabbed his laptop. There was only one way he knew to occupy his time, so he pulled up Google and started his plan.

$\sim$

ADELE HAD DEFINITELY MADE way too many fruitcakes this year. That was for sure. Addison decided to take one of them and give it to Clay's mother, since she was sure that she'd enjoy it while taking care of his father.

Clay hadn't made an effort to get in contact, and a small part of her hoped he might be at their house. When she pulled up in her car, his truck wasn't at his house or his parents'. And she hadn't seen it at the ferry dock either, which was strange.

She knocked on the door. Clay's mother, Patricia, answered almost immediately and smiled when she saw Addison.

"Oh my goodness! Clay said you were back, Addison. I was hoping we'd see you before you left to go back to Atlanta!" she said.

"It's so good to see you, Patricia. And I think I'm staying in January Cove for the foreseeable future," Addison said as she hugged the older woman. Patricia had aged well and still had a trim figure and platinum blond hair. She'd always kept that hair color no matter how obvious it was that her natural color was nowhere near it.

"Please, come in," she said, opening the door.

Addison walked inside and was struck by how the house still looked much the same. There was a new sofa, but the decor was trapped in a time from long ago.

"I brought you one of Mom's fruitcakes," Addison said, holding out the plastic wrapped mound of sugar.

"Oh, wonderful! Adele makes the best fruitcakes in town," Patricia said. And then there was an uncomfortable silence as the two women sat across from each other.

"I guess you've heard about my predicament?" Addison finally said.

"Your divorce? Yes, I've heard. Clay said the guy is a jerk," Patricia said with a sad smile.

"Very true," Addison said. "And you've heard about this?" she said, pointing to her belly.

"I did," she said softly. "And I'm so happy for you, Addison."

"Thank you."

"Can I say something?" Patricia asked.

"Of course."

"Don't give up on Clay just yet."

"Excuse me?" Addison said, taken aback by his mother's words.

"Addison, he's always been fond of you, even when your brothers told him to cut it out," she laughed. "But Clay is a serious soul. He believes in love, and he stands by those he loves. I'm just saying not to count him out yet..."

"Patricia, I appreciate that but this mess isn't Clay's to clean up. He deserves a woman without so much baggage."

"You let him decide how much baggage he's willing to carry," she said softly. Before Addison could respond, Clay's father appeared in the room. He looked confused and much thinner than Addison remembered.

"Pat, have you seen the dog?" he said, totally ignoring Addison.

"No, dear. I think he went for a walk," she said before whispering to Addison that they didn't have a dog.

"Who's this?" he asked, pointing at Addison.

"This is Addison Parker, dear," she said loudly. "You remember her, don't you?"

"Oh, yes, Addison. My, she's grown up, hasn't she? Did Clay finally marry her?" Addison's heart skipped a beat.

"No, honey. Addison is married to someone else."

"Well, that's too bad. Clay sure did love her," he said before shuffling back into the kitchen. Addison was left speechless for once in her life.

CHAPTER 11

*C*hristmas at the Parker house was legendary, and Addison was enjoying it more this year with everyone around. Somehow, she'd successfully managed to stay in the house and not go looking for Clay to see if she could get another kiss out of him.

But she'd thought about it. A lot.

It was Christmas Day and everyone had breakfast together. They enjoyed hash browns, scrambled eggs and coffee along with biscuits and gravy. Addison was stuffed, and the baby was moving like crazy. She considered it a Christmas gift that she could now feel her baby moving, giving her the knowledge that things were okay in there.

Being alone and pregnant was hard. She longed to have a husband who cared about her and their baby. Someone to rub her back at night, make her put her feet up, run a hot bath for her. Someone to care. She'd never had that, even when Jim was at his "best".

After breakfast, the family gathered in the living

room and exchanged presents. It was a happy time with kids running everywhere and laughter filling the room. She smell of cinnamon and pine wafted around the room, but was in jeopardy of being overpowered by the homemade apple pie cooking in the oven.

And Addison couldn't help but feel a void. She really wished Clay had come.

~

"THIS ROOM ISN'T big enough for all these people," Aaron said with a laugh as he sat beside Addison on the fireplace.

"I'm starting to wonder if we'll be able to fit the new baby in here next year!"

"Wow. That's hard to believe. This time next year, you'll be a mother."

"I know. Someone will call me mother. Crazy!" she said giggling.

"You'll be a great mom, Addy."

"Thanks, Aaron. And you'll be a great Daddy. I guess you already are."

Aaron looked over at Tyler, all hyped on Christmas cookies he swiped before breakfast, playing with his new firetruck. It warmed Aaron's heart. He really did think of Tyler as his son.

Then he looked at Tessa who was sitting with Adele laughing. Her beautiful eyes lit up the room as she quickly found him in the crowd and smiled. God, her smile went straight through his soul. All he knew in that moment was that he wanted to spend all of his

Christmases with Tessa and Tyler. He wanted to build a family with her.

She was nothing like Natalie. Brad had been right. Love means trusting someone, and he was going to put his trust into Tessa.

～

It was almost lunchtime, and Addison needed to freshen up. She went upstairs to her room to brush her teeth and touch up her makeup before they did family Christmas pictures in the afternoon.

When she walked into her room, she noticed a wrapped gift sitting on her bed. The tag had her name on it, but she didn't recognize the handwriting as her mother's.

She sat down and did what she always did; she opened the gift before the card. It was a beautiful set of handmade ABC blocks, intricately carved and painted in vibrant blues, reds and yellows. Someone had obviously put a great deal of time into making them, and Addison wondered where a person could buy them around town. They didn't sell any handmade toys in January Cove that she knew of.

When she opened the card, it took her breath away.

Dear Addy,

I'm sorry I left you standing on the beach at the time you needed me most. You're going to make the most incredible mother. You're a strong woman, and I admire what you're doing. I hope you'll forgive me.

Merry Christmas.

Clay

She was stunned. Had he made these in the last two days? While she was thinking of him and wishing he'd call or come by, he was doing this?

Just then, she heard the doorbell ring. How romantic! It had to be Clay coming to see her. She moved as quickly as a pregnant woman could, bounding down the stairs and right past her mother who was attempting to answer the door.

She swung it open, ready to hug Clay and say she was sorry. Instead, Harrison Gibbs was standing in front of her.

"Mr. Gibbs? Did we have an appointment?" she stammered, disappointed that Clay wasn't the one standing in front of her.

"No..." he started.

"Well, no offense, but it's Christmas Day and my family..."

"Addison, I invited Harrison over for Christmas lunch," Adele said, pulling the door back and smiling at him. Addison bit her lips.

"Sorry, I didn't know... I thought..." she stammered.

"No big deal, Addison. Today isn't about business. My kids are out of town, so your mother was nice enough to invite me to lunch," he smiled. She was starting to feel like a third wheel with these two. But it was kind of cute.

Harrison came inside and the family gathered around the table for the traditional blessing. Addison closed her eyes and silently thanked God for all the people who were rallying around her and the baby. She thanked God for the blessing of a healthy pregnancy so far, her brothers, her mother and even for Clay's friendship. She had a lot to be thankful for this Christmas season, and she intended to start the new year as a new person.

～

A FEW DAYS AFTER CHRISTMAS, Harrison came back over to the house, but this time it was for business. Adele was at her real estate office, so Addison met with him alone.

"Thanks for meeting with me today, Addison. We have lots to go over."

"Good. I'm ready to get this over with soon," she said, shutting the front door and pointing him toward the kitchen table again.

He spread some papers out in front of him. "First, we've got the goods on Jim."

She smiled. "Oh yeah?"

"Look at this," Harrison said, pulling out his iPad and opening a video. It was a bit grainy and in black and white, but it showed Jim and Tiffani in an elevator somewhere. They were all over each other, kissing and going further than one would in an elevator - if they had any class.

"When was this?"

"It was about six months before you left him. Plenty of time before your 'indiscretion'," he said, using air quotes.

"Was this at his office?" she asked, watching the

video again. It was amazing how unattached she was. There was no pain in her heart watching her own husband kiss another woman because she didn't love him. She wasn't sure she'd ever really loved him, though she'd tried as hard as she knew how.

"No. This was at a fancy hotel in downtown San Francisco when he took a business trip."

"He never took a trip there. What's the date on this?" she asked, answering her own question when she saw it stamped on the video. "Wow."

"What?"

"That was our wedding anniversary. He canceled our plans because he said his Uncle Ned, who lives in Montana, had died. He told me there was no need to come, so he went alone."

"Hmm…. Maybe we need to see if old Uncle Ned even died?"

"Yep. How's that going to look if he used a family member's fake death to screw his ditzy secretary?" she said with a chuckle. "What an idiot."

"I've got more news for you too."

"Okay…"

"I spoke with your attorney. She's aware of this information, but I also had her get into contact with the father of your baby. He still wants no contact with the baby, and he's signed over his parental rights, Addison." He pushed the stack of paperwork over to her.

Addison's eyes filled with tears. She didn't really know why as she hadn't planned on him being involved anyway, but it still made her sad for the baby. Being rejected wasn't easy for anyone, and one day she'd have to explain that to her child.

"Thanks, Mr. Gibbs. I'm glad to have that part over with, but it's still sad that a man would deny his own child," she said, wiping a stray tear from her cheek. Harrison handed her his handkerchief. Who still carried those things?

"It is, but you know you'll find love again, Addison. Real love. And that man will love your child as if it was his own."

She smiled and handed him back the handkerchief. "You think so, huh?"

"I think you know a friend of mine," he said, raising one eyebrow.

"I do?"

"Clay Hampton. He's actually my god son."

Addison was shocked. Of course, she shouldn't have been. Practically everyone in their small town knew each other.

"Wow. I had no idea. I've known Clay my whole life," she said. "He's a great guy."

"That he is," Harrison said with a smile. "And he really likes you, Addison."

"Excuse me?"

"Look, I'm an old man and I don't have a lot of time for beating around the bush. Plus, I'm a private investigator and ex-cop, so I know how to read people. He loves you, Addison. And he has for a long time."

"Mr. Gibbs..."

"Please call me Harrison."

"Okay. Harrison, this whole trip back home has

been a lot to take in. Add to that a terrible divorce and a baby, and well, my mind just can't take much more."

"Do you love him?" he asked.

"I don't know him like that. He's always been my friend, almost like a brother."

"Don't lie, Addison," he said chuckling. "Remember I used to grill people for hours in tiny rooms with lights above their heads. You're no better at lying than a two-bit thief."

"Gee, thanks," she said crossing her arms. "Guess my plans of becoming a thief have been dashed." This guy really had some gall.

"I just want to see Clay happy. And truthfully, I want to see you happy too. I like your mother, you can plainly see that. I know she'd be delighted if you had someone who would love you and that baby and take care of you."

"I think you're jumping the gun here, Harrison. First, I'm not even divorced yet. Second, no one said Clay would love my baby."

"Actually, Clay told me that, Addison." You could've heard a pin drop in the room.

"What?" she said, her mouth gaping open.

"Look, Addison, your father was one of my best friends. He was such a good, decent, family man. Clay reminds me of your Dad. He loves you, I know he does. And I think you know he does. All I'm saying is that you deserve to be happy and to have someone to love you, and I think Clay could be that person if you give him a chance."

"Can I ask you something?"

"Sure."

"What was my Dad like? I don't remember him, and all I have to go on is the memories of my family members."

"Oh, your Dad was a great guy. Super funny. Always the life of the party. Told the silliest jokes and always played pranks on his friends."

"Really?" Addison found herself smiling at the thought of her Dad being such a clown. "I'm the funny one in my family. At least that's what I'm told. Of course, I haven't felt so funny lately."

"I know one thing for sure. When you were born, your Dad was over the moon. He finally had his girl after three boys before you. He loved his boys, but he doted on you like you were a real life princess. Told me that he was going to sit at the front door with his shot gun when you started dating. Figured he'd clean it while he met the boys who came calling." Harrison chuckled. "I believe he'd have done it."

"I bet," Addison said smiling. "I miss him even though I don't remember him."

"You know, he met Clay a couple of times."

"He did?"

"Right before he died. Clay was just a kid, of course, but your father liked him enough to take him and Kyle fishing once. They went down to the pier, in fact."

"The pier where Clay runs the ferry?"

"The very same one. It's one of the reasons why Clay decided to run the ferry, Addison. That place has memories for him."

"He never told me he met my Dad."

"Probably didn't want to dig up old wounds. Well, I've got to go to another appointment now. Some woman wanting to dig up dirt on her cheating husband," he said with a wink. "Keeps me busy."

"I'm sure it does!" she said as she walked him to the door.

"I hope I didn't pry too much, Addison. I just care about you and Clay."

"I know you do. And thank you."

With that, Addison watched Harrison walk to his car and drive away. And then she wondered what to do with this newfound information.

～

ADDISON WENT BACK to work the next morning with renewed hope that her life would get back on track soon. She would talk to Clay and hopefully at least preserve their friendship. She would hear from her attorney soon about the new settlement offer they'd be making to Jim's attorney. She'd also see her doctor again soon to check on the baby.

The holidays had passed, so she'd also be helping Jenna prepare for her upcoming wedding. There was lots to do, and most of it would be a welcome distraction from the worries that floated through her mind each day.

"So, has Jenna shown you the bridesmaids dresses?" Rebecca asked as she cut the freshly made poundcake.

"No, not yet. Are they awful?" Addison asked with a laugh.

"Not too bad. No puffy sleeves, at least," Rebecca said with a giggle.

The chime of the door caused them both to turn their heads. Rebecca wasn't alarmed by who was standing there, but then again she'd never seen Jim.

"Dear God, what are you doing here?" Addison said through gritted teeth. "Jim, get out or I'll call the police."

Rebecca stepped around the counter. "You need to leave."

"Relax, ladies. I'm just here for a cup of coffee and a civil conversation with my wife." He gave Rebecca his best attorney smile.

"You don't know how to have a civil conversation," Addison said with her arms crossed. She stayed behind the counter.

"I'll be good. I promise." He held up his right hand like he was swearing in a courtroom, but it meant nothing. He'd also sworn before God that he'd be faithful and that didn't happen.

"It's okay, Rebecca. I can handle him. We'll just step outside since this is a place of business."

"Addy, you can stay…"

Addison waved her hand. "It'll be fine."

She followed Jim out to the sidewalk and pulled her coat around her.

"Look, Addison, we need to discuss this settlement like rational adults."

"Rational? Since when were you ever rational?"

He took in a deep breath and pursed his lips. She knew she was getting to him.

"The settlement that your attorney submitted is ridiculous. You're basically asking for half of everything I own."

"Everything you own? Um, I believe I own the same amount you do, Jim."

"You did nothing to earn that money!" he snapped. "You were a worthless piece of baggage that I carried for all those years. You don't deserve a dime."

"Is that what you told Tiffani in the elevator? At the fancy schmancy hotel in San Fran?" she said with her eyes wide and a smile on her face. Jim's jaw dropped.

"What?"

"On our anniversary, Jim? Really? Very classy."

"How do you... Wait. What?" He still hadn't put two and two together.

"Also, how's uncle Ned?"

"Huh?" he continued to stammer.

"Oh, yeah, Jimbo. I forgot to tell you that I have the goods on you. I'm not worried about my reputation anymore, sweetheart, because I don't intend to ever go back to my old life or my old career. People here know the real me. They know who I am, and they wouldn't listen to you anyway. But I can guarantee that your colleagues in Atlanta would love to get the scoop on who you really are. Give me a reason, Jim. Just give me a reason," she said, her finger pointed in his face. For the first time, she stared him down and let him know she wasn't going to back down anymore.

"You're a bitch!" he said. "I married you so I'd look good, having the whole stay at home wife thing. But you aren't who I married. Thank God I'm almost rid of you."

"The feeling's mutual. Trust me. Now, get out of here." She turned and started to walk inside, but he just couldn't let her go. He grabbed her arm and twirled her around.

"That bastard baby of yours will never have a life. You should choose adoption..."

He never got to finish that sentence because the next thing he saw was the front of Clay's fist as it crashed down on his formerly perfect nose.

~

ADDISON HAD NEVER BAILED anyone out of jail before. Until today.

Clay had knocked Jim out cold, leaving him with a broken nose and one black eye. Addison couldn't help but laugh on the inside, but thankfully she'd held it together on the outside.

After paying the bail, Clay walked out of the small county jail holding a plastic bag with his wallet, keys and whatever else he had in his pants pockets.

"You okay?" she asked, crinkling her nose, as he met her on the sidewalk.

"Well, I've been better," he said with a sad laugh. "The question is, how are you? Did he hurt you before I got there?" he asked, touching her arm where Jim had touched her. Amazing how two men's touches could be so vastly different.

"I'm fine," she said, putting her other hand over his. He let go.

"He tried to press assault charges, but Rebecca and another eye witness told the officer that I was getting him off of you. In the end, Jim was too big of a coward to proceed with it because he knew it would hurt his reputation."

"No surprise there," she said as they walked toward her car. "Come on, I'll give you a ride home."

"That's okay. I had a couple of my friends bring my car so I'd have it when I got out."

"Oh. Okay. By the way, thanks for the baby gift. You didn't have to do that. It must have been a lot of work..."

"You're welcome. It was no big deal." He wouldn't look at her, and it was making her uneasy. Had Harrison Gibbs gotten it all wrong?

"Are you angry with me or something?"

"No."

"You know what, you're all hat and no cattle, Clay Hampton!" she screeched a little louder than she'd planned.

"Excuse me?" he said, turning to look at her.

"You said all those nice things, and you claim not to be upset about my pregnancy, but you're barely speaking to me right now. When the chips are down, you're bolting yet again!"

"Really? That's what you think? I just punched your sorry husband out and went to jail for a few hours, but I'm 'bolting'?"

"Just admit it. You think I'm a whore just like Jim

does!" she said pointing at him. She knew as soon as she'd said it, she'd said the wrong thing. He looked pale and shell shocked. He'd saved her from Jim, at least in his mind, and now she was being ungrateful.

"Sweetie, I'm not in the business of protecting whores. But if that's what you think, then I guess I'll see you around," he said as he got into his car and drove away.

~

ADDISON DROVE by the ferry a few times over the next week, but she didn't see Clay's car. Maybe he was walking to work these days, burning off the rage he felt for her.

Amazingly, she received a signed divorce settlement from her attorney in just over a week from the time Jim had shown up. She gladly signed it and returned it to Helen, who was happy to have the case over with.

She would get half of the house they lived in together once it sold. She would also get half of their savings account and some of the retirement funds over time. All in all, she would be able to start over and raise her baby with a nice nest egg. She could even buy a house in January Cove if she wanted. Or somewhere else, although she couldn't imagine the thought of that.

Her appointment with the doctor revealed the baby's gender and she couldn't have been more excited to have a baby girl on the way. But she felt let down that she didn't have Clay to share it with.

She decided to walk past the Mallory house once

again. Maybe she'd do something crazy and make an offer on it. She could live there and run her B&B like she dreamed. Imagining the pink nursery she could have upstairs overlooking the garden, she walked as quickly as she could to see her dream home.

And there was a sold sign on it.

What? Who could've bought it so quickly? She had the money now, and her house was gone.

Dejected, she decided to find Clay and see if he knew anything about the new owners. Maybe she could negotiate to buy it from them.

As she walked up to the ferry dock, she saw some guy she didn't recognize.

"Can I help you, miss?" the older man said.

"Um, I'm looking for Clay Hampton..." she said, looking around for any sign of him.

"Oh, he's out of town for awhile."

"Out of town? When will he be back?" she asked.

"Don't know, ma'am. He just told me that he was on an open-ended vacation."

"Thanks..." she stammered before she walked back toward the road.

He'd left January Cove for the first time, and it was all because of her.

CHAPTER 12

"These aren't half bad," Rebecca said with a laugh as she spun around in the pale pink bridesmaid dress. Jenna rolled her eyes.

"Did ya'll really think I would make you look bad at my own wedding?" she asked. Each of the women shrugged their shoulders and giggled. In unison, they all said, "Maybe."

"Well, I'd appreciate it if someone could pry me out of this dress and get me a bigger size!" Addison said, laughing so hard that she feared she'd bust the dress wide open. "I need an adjustable one," she said to the attendant. The women all burst into hysterical laughter.

It had been weeks since she last saw Clay, but Addison was picking up her life and moving forward. She had more to worry about with a baby girl on the way.

After finally relenting, she opted to stay with her mother at least until the baby was a few months old. So

Adele had started to work on the nursery, and she was going overboard, as usual.

The whole room was being repainted, the floors sanded and all new decor had been ordered. Addison just sat back and smiled, letting her mother have all the fun.

Planning Jenna and Kyle's wedding had been a lot of fun too, with the exception of knowing that Clay would be driving the ferry boat and attending as a groomsman. She dreaded seeing him again after the way she'd talked to him before.

After her bridesmaid dress escapade, she met up with her brother, Jackson, for lunch.

"So, how goes the dress shopping?" he asked as he bit into a hamburger.

"Pretty good except my expanding girth is a challenge," she said smiling.

"Well, for good reason. I can't wait to meet my niece. I'm gonna spoil her rotten." And she knew he would. "Any ideas on a name yet?"

"I was thinking of Anna Grace."

"I like it," he said, taking a sip of his soda.

"So... Have you seen Clay lately?" she asked, trying to sound nonchalant.

"No, but I heard he just came back to town or something. Said he needed a break." Jackson was eying her closely. "Something going on with you two?"

"Nah. Just wondering. Hadn't seen him around."

"Addy, I'm not an idiot. I've seen the way he looks at you, and I've seen the way you look at him. He broke Jim's nose for you."

"Well... I... uh..."

"Pregnancy got your tongue?"

"Very funny."

"If you like Clay, why not just admit it?" he asked.

"Because you've done everything in your power to keep him from even looking at me for years."

"Is that what he told you?" Jackson asked with a wide grin.

"Maybe."

"Well, I'm your big brother. What was I supposed to do?"

"Let me make my own decisions?"

"You decided on Jim. Not a feather in your cap, sis."

"You're a regular comedian today," she said sarcastically. "Besides, he's angry at me for being a jerk after I bailed him out. I don't think he wants to hang out with me anymore."

"Doubt that. He's drooled over you since you were a teenager, Addy. If you like Clay, then tell him. That boy can't stand to be led on. He needs to know how you feel. Otherwise, he runs for cover."

"Really?"

"He's a big guy, but he's got a big heart too. Jeez, I can't believe I just said that..."

"You're becoming a softie, bro," she said as she stood and kissed him on the head. "Thanks."

"Where are you going?" he called after her.

"To find that big hearted man!" she yelled back as she walked down the street toward the ferry.

As she approached the ferry dock, she saw him. Wearing a long sleeve navy blue shirt and form fitting jeans, she ogled him for just a bit too long. He turned around and looked at her.

"Are you checking me out?" he asked with a hint of a smile.

"Maybe," she said, slowly walking toward him.

"You look good," he said, pointing down to her belly. "And..."

"Bigger?"

"I'm not saying that..."

"It's okay. In this case, bigger is better," she said. He nodded thoughtfully. "I'm having a girl."

"Really? That's awesome."

"Yeah, I'm excited to have a daughter."

"It's so good to see you again, Addy," he said stepping off the dock and bridging the gap between them.

"I've missed you, Clay. I'm so sorry about the way I acted at the jail. I was just going through a lot. But the divorce is over now, and I got a good settlement. I'm starting over, and I'm happy."

"I'm glad to hear that. You deserve happiness."

"Listen, I was wondering about something."

"Yeah?"

"Do you know who bought the Mallory house? I notice it's got a sold sign now and there's work being done there."

"Hmm... I don't know, but then I haven't been around much."

"Oh. Okay." She was starting to chicken out.

"Well, it was good to see you…" he started to say as he turned to head back to the ferry.

"Will you go on a date with me?" she said at the same time. Awkward.

"What did you say?"

"Nothing," she stammered as she started to walk away.

"Addy! Wait up!" he called. Once he caught up with her, he turned her to him. "Did you just ask me on date, Addison Rose Parker?"

"How do you know my middle name?"

"I've made it my business to know everything about you," he said softly. "And to answer your question, I would love to go on a date with you. A real one."

"Okay," she said, sure that her cheeks were a bright shade of crimson.

"But on one condition."

Great. A condition. "What condition?"

"That you let me plan it. The man should ask the woman on the date, and the man should plan it."

"Southern chivalry?" she said, smiling up at him.

"Of course. How about tomorrow night?"

"It's a date," she said as she backed away. "And I won't stand you up this time."

∾

ADDISON WAS EXCITED about her date with Clay, and she didn't hide that fact from her mother.

"So, Clay Hampton is your date?" Adele said.

"Yes, mother..." Addison said as she put her earrings in and checked the mirror for the sixth time.

"Well, I think that's just great."

"You do?" Addison said, surprised that her mother would be okay with her pregnant daughter dating.

"Of course. He's like a son to me. I love Clay. I couldn't have picked a better person for you to date. Besides, he's loved you for years, sweetie."

"Why didn't anyone ever tell me that?" Addison screeched out. How had she been so blind to it all those years?

"Because love has to find its own way. You can't push it. What's meant to be is meant to be."

"How many cliches can you pack into one sentence, Mom?" Addison said with a laugh as she hugged her mom's neck. "Thank you so much for everything you've been doing with the baby's room. It's much appreciated."

"It's my joy to welcome a third generation of Parker women into this family, Addy." Adele smiled and continued painting the walls of the nursery.

"Well, I'd better get ready," Addison said. "He'll be here in less than an hour."

⁓

CLAY STARED at her for a moment before handing her a small bouquet of yellow roses.

"These are my favorite!" she said, putting them up to her nose to get an early whiff of springtime.

"I know," he said softly.

"You amaze me."

"The feeling is mutual," he said with a smile. Those dimples did things to her that she couldn't mention in polite company.

"So, where are we going?"

"It's a surprise," he said with a huge grin. She nodded her head slowly.

"Okay…. Hang on a sec… Hey, Mom, can you put these in some water for me?" she yelled into the house before handing the flowers to her mother through the door. Adele shot a quick smile and wink in Clay's direction before closing the door behind them.

"Why do I feel like a teenager right now?" he asked as they walked down the steps.

He opened the door to his truck and helped her up inside. The truck wasn't overly tall, but being six months pregnant was a challenge in several ways.

As they rode down the street, Addison mused in her head about the fact that she was going on a date as a pregnant woman. Never would've expected that.

"Close your eyes," Clay said.

"What?"

"Close your eyes. Where we're going is a surprise."

"Seriously?"

"Yep. Here," he said, handing her a neck tie. She put it around her face and decided to play along.

"This is already the most interesting date I've ever had," she said laughing. "Are you driving in circles?"

"I'm just throwing you off track," he said as he turned for the tenth time.

"I'm getting vertigo!" she said with a giggle.

"Okay, fine," he said as he turned onto a road and finally stopped the car. "Stay there."

She stayed where she was until Clay opened the door and helped her out, practically lifting her from the truck and placing her gently on the ground.

"Be careful. There's some gravel on the ground," he said. "Keep your eyes covered."

He led her up some stairs and she could hear him unlocking a door. Had he brought her to his house? She tried to remember how many steps he had on his front porch. She heard him close the door and then take a deep breath.

"Okay, you can take off your mask now," he said softly. Addison reached up and pulled the tie from around her eyes, taking a couple of moments to allow her eyes to adjust again.

At first, she had no idea where she was, but it was a beautiful place with thick moldings and shiny hardwood floors. She looked at Clay who was smiling like a Cheshire cat, and then looked behind them and out the window.

The Mallory house.

"Oh my goodness, Clay. We're at the Mallory house?" she whispered.

"Why are you whispering?" he asked with a chuckle.

"Because we aren't supposed to be here. What if we get caught?" she continued whispering. "The workers were just here yesterday."

"Don't you like to live a little on the edge?" he asked as he walked toward her. "Live a little dangerously?"

"Well, obviously," she said pointing at her pregnant

belly. "But still, we should get out of here. I don't want to be the cause of you getting a reputation at the county jail!"

She started walking toward the door. "Addy?"

"Yes?" she asked, anxious to get the heck out of the Mallory house, as beautiful as it was.

"I own this place."

"What?" she said, completely baffled and confused.

"I'm the buyer." He smiled and waited for her to catch up.

"You bought this place? When? Why?"

"How 'bout I catch you up over dinner?" he said, taking her hand and pulling her toward the kitchen at the back of the house. They dodged circular saws and other tools as they made their way to the large kitchen. It had been totally renovated along with the adjoining breakfast area.

Her mouth gaped open when she looked at the work that had been done so far. The granite counter-tops were top of the line, and the tile backsplash was perfect for the time period. The original floors had been shined up, and the cabinetry restored to its former glory.

He pulled out a chair for her at the mahogany reproduction table and sat across from her. On the table was catered food from the local Italian restaurant, Bel Cibo.

"Okay, Clay Hampton, start explaining." She smiled at him as he started making their plates.

"Well, I started the purchase process right after we talked about it on the ferry that day. You were so hopeless, thinking you wouldn't get a settlement, but I knew this was your dream. And your dreams are my dreams, Addy. So I made an offer, did some haggling and got it closed. Then I got my guys working on it, quietly of course."

"I don't know what to say…" she stammered, staring at him in awe.

"Say you'll decorate it. I had the kitchen mostly done because I wanted our first official date to be here, in this place, but I want your stamp on it."

She grinned. "Seriously?"

"And when you're done with that, I want you to open that B&B. Here."

"What?" she said, dropping her fork.

"I bought this place for you, Addy. I was hoping you'd live here with the baby, and run it as a B&B."

"I can't let you do this for me, Clay…"

"It's my money, Addy. I want us to be partners. I'll still run the ferry, but this can be my sideline. I'll keep my house, and you can live here."

"Why are you doing this?" she asked softly.

"Because I love you, Addy, and I have for years. And it's okay if you don't love me yet, but just know I intend to do everything I can to change that," he said with a wink. "Now, let's eat. I'm starving."

She stood up and walked around the table, pulling his arm up. Standing in front of her, she realized how tall he was. He towered over her petite - well, formerly petite - frame, but she felt so safe with him.

She wrapped her arms around his midsection and put her head on his chest, closing her eyes and breathing him in. "Thank you…" she whispered. "No one has ever done anything like this for me before."

"You're special, Addy. I want you to believe that," he said, his lips pressed to the top of her head.

"When I see myself through your eyes, I start to believe it."

"Good. Now, let's eat so I can take you to see the rest of the house," he said. She grinned up at him.

"You're too good to be true, Clay Hampton."

"You haven't seen anything yet," he whispered. Before she could respond, his lips pressed against hers and she forgot every word in the English language.

~

FOR THE NEXT FEW WEEKS, Clay and Addison worked side by side. She planned the decor of the new B&B while he directed the rehab crew.

Anytime he could pull her into a dark closet for a snuggle or a kiss, he did. Her belly was enlarging by the day, and she felt like she would pop at any time, but she still had a good six weeks left. In fact, she was due to have Anna Grace about three weeks before her brother's wedding in early May.

They hadn't talked a lot about their "relationship" yet, or whatever it was, and she hadn't told him she loved him. It felt kind of strange, having this wonderful man do so much for her and not being able to reciprocate yet. But Addison didn't want to rush into anything. She wanted to take her time, for once in her life, and enjoy the ride.

"Hey, beautiful," he whispered into her ear from behind as he slid his hands around her waist. He had big hands, which led to other musings in her mind, but she wasn't about to go there. She was far too pregnant to be intimate with Clay. It wasn't the way she wanted him to see her their first time. Truly, the whole thing was a bit of a rush - falling in love without the physical act of sex. It made her feel treasured and cherished for who she was instead of what she could give him.

"Well, hello… I thought you were running the ferry today," she said as she turned her head and stole a kiss.

"I got a substitute today because I have something special to show you."

He walked her to the front of the house and out onto the porch. The beginning of spring had brought with it warmth and a cool breeze. It was her favorite time of year.

There was a big item on the porch, draped with a white cloth. Clay pulled the cloth off in one motion revealing a handmade wooden sign. It said "Addy's Inn".

"It's beautiful!" she squealed. They hadn't even decided on a name for the place, but once again he'd surprised her. "Did you make this?"

"Yes," he said, smiling at her. "I've been working on it at night for weeks."

She hugged him tightly. "It's starting to seem real."

"It is real, Addy. This is going to be your place. Your new start. Your baby's new home." He brushed her hair behind her ear, grazing her cheek with his thumb.

"I'm so excited! I can't wait to have my first guest!

Do you think your mom might give me her blueberry pancake recipe? I'd love to serve that here."

"I'm sure she won't mind," he said laughing.

"We can call them 'Patty Cakes,'" she said clapping. "Isn't that cute?" Clay smiled at her excitement, even over the naming of pancakes.

Suddenly, Addison was overcome with pain. It was a searing pain that didn't feel like the Braxton Hicks contractions she'd started having a couple of weeks before. She doubled over, clutching her stomach and groaning, hardly able to speak.

"Addy? Addy?" Clay said as he knelt down in front of her. "Talk to me. What's happening?"

"It hurts!" she screamed, tears streaming down her face. "Something's wrong."

CHAPTER 13

"Can I please see her now?" Clay begged the nurse.

"I'm sorry, sir. Unless you're family or her husband, I can't allow it."

Clay felt helpless. It was too early. She still had six weeks left. He didn't know if babies could survive that early. He thought they could, but what if he was wrong? Dear God, why hadn't he paid better attention in health class?

"Clay!" Adele said as she rushed down the hall, Addy's brothers right behind her. "What happened? Is Addison okay?"

"I don't know anything. They won't talk to me since I'm not the father… or the husband."

"I'll go get some answers," Jackson said, moving past them and down the hall.

"It was so scary. We were just standing on the porch talking when she suddenly doubled over. I got her here as fast as I could…"

"I know you did everything you could for her, Clay. None of us question your love for Addison," Adele said with a sad smile on her face.

"Can a baby make it this early? Please say yes," Clay said, holding Adele's hands.

"Yes. Absolutely. We just have to hope for the best."

A few moments later, Jackson returned.

"She's stable right now, but her labor has started. Her water broke right after she got here, so they need to deliver the baby within twenty-four hours. They can't stop the contractions, so she could start delivering soon."

"Did they say if she's dilated?" Rebecca asked as she walked up to the group, with Jenna and Tessa behind her.

"Yes. She's six centimeters already. Progressing very quickly."

"Oh my God..." Tessa said.

"Clay Hampton?" a nurse called. Clay shot up like a rocket and almost ran into her.

"That's me."

"Addison would like you to come into the room. Please follow me..." Clay looked back at Adele and the rest of the family. They smiled and gave a thumbs up, but he could see the worry in their faces. He was worried too.

He entered the room and wasn't prepared for what he saw. Addison's face was streaked with tears, her eyes puffy and red. Her face contorted in pain as a contraction came right as he walked up to her bedside. She reached for his hand and squeezed the life out of it. How could someone so tiny almost break his big hand?

"They're coming with my epidural…" she mumbled through panting breaths. "They promised!" she yelled, trying to get the nurse's attention.

"Take slow, deep breaths…" Clay said, trying to mimic the breathing he'd seen on movies and TV shows before. He should have taken Lamaze classes with her, but she had insisted she didn't need classes to teach her how to breathe.

"I'm trying…" she said, tears rolling from her eyes. A moment later, the contraction had subsided. She just looked so pitiful, her small frame crumpled over in the bed. "I'm so tired."

"I know you are, sweetie, but you're doing great."

"It's too early, Clay."

"Women have babies a lot earlier than this, and they're fine. Anna Grace is going to be fine. She's going to be beautiful, just like her mother," he said, leaning up to plant a kiss on her forehead.

"I love you," she whispered, barely loud enough for him to hear.

"What?"

"I planned to tell you today, but then this whole thing happened. Not the romantic way I planned to say it, but I want you to know that I love you, Clay Hampton." He stared at her and almost teared up himself.

"I love you too, Addison Rose. And I love Anna Grace too," he said smiling.

"You haven't met her yet!" she giggled.

"Well, she's a part of you and that makes me love her."

"But she's also a part of someone else, Clay. Doesn't that bother you?"

"Nope. Not a bit."

"You amaze me again, mister," she said, reaching up and pulling his head down toward her. His lips barely brushed hers when another contraction clamped down on her body, forcing a loud cry from her lips.

Nurses rushed in, and Clay was terrified for a moment. "Addison, your contractions are coming closer and closer, so we need to check you again."

Clay stepped to the head of the bed so the nurses could work in private.

"Sweetie, you're almost at nine already. This baby's coming. We're going to get the doctor to let you start pushing..." the nurse said.

"No! Where's my epidural?" she cried. Addison wasn't at all interested in a natural childbirth. She'd said it all throughout the pregnancy.

"Honey, it's too late for that," the older African American nurse said. "This baby's coming whether we want her to or not. She's kind of stubborn, that one."

Clay smiled. *Just like her mother*, he thought.

"I'll go get your mom..." Clay said.

"No..." Addison said. "I want you."

"Me? But Addy, I think your mom would be more help..."

"Please stay. Hold my hand," she said as she reached up. Clay took a chair at the head of the bed and held her hand, rubbing her forehead with his other hand.

"And stay up here," she whispered. "The first time a guy sees a woman's... you know... should not be during childbirth." Clay laughed.

"Fine with me. But does this mean I'll get to see your... you know... in the future?" he whispered in her ear.

"I'd say your odds are really, really good on that one, Mr. Hampton," she said before another contraction hit and took her breath away.

The doctor came in and checked her. "Addison, you're ready to push, okay?" she said.

The next few minutes were frantic as Clay watched the woman he loved struggle with pains he couldn't stop. It was hard to watch, so he just held her hand and occasionally pressed his lips to the top of her head, trying everything he knew to just let her know he was there.

And then he heard the noise that made it all worth it. A loud set of lungs let loose a cry that probably could've been heard down the street. Addison started to laugh and then cry herself, and Clay felt a few stray tears on his face too.

The doctor put the baby on Addison's chest. She looked perfect. She had all her fingers and toes. Good color. Strong lungs. She was tiny, as to be expected, but seemed otherwise in good condition.

"Hi, Anna Grace..." Addison said softly.

"She's beautiful, just like her Mommy," Clay said, his chin resting on Addison's shoulder. Maybe she had some of her father's features, but he couldn't see those. All he saw was Addison's adorable nose and pouty lips.

"We need to clean her up and check some vitals," the nurse said, removing the baby from Addison's chest. She looked up at Clay.

"Thank you."

"I didn't do anything," he said, wiping her sweat filled hair from her forehead.

"You've done everything to turn my life around, Clay. I love you."

"We're in this together. I love you too." He wound his pinky finger around hers and together they watched little Anna Grace from across the room.

～

"IT'S A SCREAMING BABY GIRL!" Clay yelled when he burst through the doors into the waiting room. Adele started crying and clapping, so excited about her brand new grand baby.

"How's Addison?" Jackson asked, always the protective older brother.

"She did great. They're just getting her set up in a room now, and Anna Grace is being checked out. They don't even think she'll need to stay in the NICU for long. She screamed bloody murder as soon as she came out," he laughed.

"Oh, that's wonderful. I know Addison is exhausted," Adele said. Clay nodded his head.

"Ya'll can see her soon, though. She can't wait to show you her new daughter," he said with a smile.

～

"My God, she looks just like you, Addison," Rebecca said as she finally got her turn to hold little Anna Grace. She was a small baby, just over 5.5 pounds, but she was gorgeous. With a tuft of dark hair, she truly looked like she belonged to Clay and Addison together.

"She looks just like her Mommy which means I'm going to have to beat some guy off with a stick one day," Clay said without thinking. Everyone looked at him, including Addison who had her mouth hanging open.

"Planning ahead a little there, buddy?" she said.

"Always," he said.

While everyone was oohing and ahing over the new baby, Jackson waved his hand at Clay and asked him to come out into the hall.

Jackson crossed his arms and looked at his friend intently. "You love my sister?"

"I do," Clay admitted. "I have for a long time."

"You gonna love that baby?"

"I already do."

"Good," Jackson said with a hint of a smile. "I'm gonna let her make her own choice about you, Clay Hampton, but don't make me sorry I let this happen."

Clay wanted to argue about the whole "let this happen" statement - as if Jackson had all that power - but he decided to "let" his friend win on this one. He got the ultimate prize anyway - Addison and Anna Grace.

Clay threw his arm around Jackson as they walked back toward the room. "And who knows, we might just be real brothers one day!"

Jackson put him in a headlock because that's what "real brothers" do, right?

~

ADDISON STARED at her new baby daughter who was sleeping soundly next to her in the hospital crib. She was exhausted from giving birth, but glad it was over. Anna Grace was perfect from head to toe. The doctors couldn't believe the set of lungs she had on her being born six weeks early, but she was a miracle straight from God in Addison's mind.

Her other miracle was snoozing peacefully in the chair on the other side of her, still holding her hand as he had most of the day. She couldn't have asked for a better partner to share her delivery with, or her life for that matter.

As she sat there, looking back and forth at her two miracles, Addison reflected on how her life had changed in the last few months. She'd left her cheating husband, made a mistake with a new man, gotten pregnant, moved back to January Cove, found the love of her life who had always been there in the first place, started a new business adventure and given birth.

And yet she was as peaceful as she'd ever felt in her life. She was home.

*A*ddison watched her boyfriend dancing with their new baby daughter. He swayed back and forth under the big tent while wedding guests milled about, congratulating Kyle and Jenna on their marriage.

Watching her mother dance with Harrison Gibbs cracked her up. Something about seeing her own mom falling in love both warmed her heart and creeped her out. They hadn't become "serious", according to Adele, but they definitely spent a lot of time together.

It had been a beautiful wedding, and Addison was so happy for them both. Jenna and Kyle had found each other young, ended up apart and then found each other all over again. They were meant to be. Just like her and Clay.

He loved Anna Grace with all his heart. In the nine weeks since she'd given birth, Clay had fallen completely in love with the baby which only made Addison fall more in love with him.

She was still living at her mother's house, using the brand new nursery they decorated together. But the Mallory house - renamed Addy's Inn - was set to open in a few weeks and she would be moving there with her new daughter. The thought both thrilled and terrified her. Being a single mother alone in a big house was a little scary, but she knew Clay would always be there watching over her.

She longed for her own family one day. She wanted to get married again and maybe even have more kids - with an epidural this time! She couldn't imagine spending her life with anyone else but Clay, and that was something she never could've said about Jim.

Addison hadn't allowed anyone to even keep the baby yet, but tonight was the night. She was letting her mother babysit overnight while she and Clay finally got some time alone. Between all the diaper changing and feeding, they had fallen right into the new parent routine but hadn't really had a chance to date. Tonight was date night.

Clay was constantly at the Parker house, helping to feed and change the baby. Truth be told, he was better at changing diapers than she was. In the evenings, he would come over just to rock baby Anna Grace to sleep, usually sitting on the front porch with her as they flowed back and forth on the old porch swing.

"We're heading out," Kyle said to Addison as he and Jenna prepared to board the ferry and head off on their Honeymoon to St. Augustine, Florida. That also meant that Clay and Addison would board the ferry too.

Addison's heart ached a little at the thought of leaving her baby on the island with her mother, but she desperately needed some "adult time" with her man.

"Bye, sweetie," Addison said as she forced Clay to hand the baby to Adele. He did so reluctantly. Addison whispered in his ear.

"I'll make it worth your while if you let her go..."

Clay quickly kissed Anna Grace goodbye and grabbed Addison's hand as they sprinted to the ferry like teenagers.

"Congratulations, you guys," Addison said to Kyle and Jenna as the ferry docked. Clay handed the reins over to his substitute, Howard Mertry, so he could pick the wedding party up in another hour or so.

"Thanks for everything, man," Kyle said to Clay as he shook his hand.

"You're welcome. Anytime."

They watched Kyle and Jenna drive away in their decorated car, complete with tin cans dangling from the bumper and "Just Hitched" written on the back window.

"So, Miss Addison Parker, are you ready for a real, adult date?" he asked.

"I'm more than ready, Mr. Clay Hampton," she cooed as they walked arm in arm down the street.

"Do you think we'll ever get hitched?" he asked.

"Honey, let's just get through tonight and then we'll worry about that," she said with a giggle.

"You still going to make it worth my while?" he asked with an eyebrow cocked.

"I guess you'll have to be the judge of that," she said smiling up at him. He scooped her up in his arms.

"All I know is that this has so been worth the wait."

~

TO GET a list of Rachel Hanna's books, visit www. RachelHannaAuthor.com.

Made in United States
North Haven, CT
06 August 2022

22360029R00107